# AN EASTER PROMISE

A E RYECART

To find out more about the author visit:

www.aeryecart.com

Disclaimer

*For Mark*

*Writing a book is a lone endeavour, but the finished product is a team effort. Beta readers, editors, cover artists and more. . . thank you.*

*But I'll end where I started, with Mark, for being unstinting in your support and encouragement.*

# CHAPTER ONE

Jack stole a glance at Rory, next to him in the passenger seat, before he indicated to turn left.

"There's nothing to worry about, honestly. You'll love them, and they'll love you. And it's only five days." Five days of the De Lacy family and everything that came with them. "If it all gets too much, we can come home early," Jack added.

"No."

They'd stopped at traffic lights, and Rory turned to Jack.

"This trip isn't just about me; it's about you too. You haven't seen your family for ages. Of course I'm nervous about meeting them, but I'm not going to run away."

Rory's chin tilted up in defiance, his chestnut brown eyes glittering with determination. Jack's heart soared. He was so proud of Rory and of how far he'd come since he'd found him huddled, freezing cold and homeless, on his doorstep just days before Christmas. In a rash act of charity, he'd taken the grubby, hungry boy in, offering no more than a brief respite from London's snow-bound streets. A hot drink had turned into a meal, then a place to sleep safe from the streets for the night. It had turned into two, three nights, and more, and Rory had never left.

It had been four months since Rory had stumbled into Jack's life and changed it out of recognition. It felt like a breath away and eons at the same time. Jack couldn't remember a past before Rory or imagine a future without him.

"I mean it. If my family are too overwhelming, we leave. No argument."

"I know you mean it, and *I mean* to prove you wrong."

The blast of a horn directly behind them and the gesticulation from the baseball-capped driver in the rusty white van made them jump. The lights had changed without them noticing, and Jack slammed the car into first gear, overrevved, and stalled. Rory sniggered, and Jack gave him a mock glare, before they moved forward, away from the city and toward the house nestled deep in the Devonshire hills.

The nearer they got, the more Rory's stomach knotted. He was determined not to screw up this first visit to Jack's parents. The problem was, Jack's parents weren't plain old Mr and Mrs De Lacy, but Sir Roger and Lady Diana. They're good people and ordinary despite everything, Jack had told him time and time again in an attempt, Rory knew, to quell his nerves.

Yes, they were ordinary if *ordinary* meant living in a grand manor house, holding hereditary titles, and owning most of the village they lived in, plus a dozen others scattered across wild, windswept Dartmoor. Whatever Jack said, no matter how much he played them down, the De Lacys were not ordinary, everyday country folk – especially to somebody who'd grown up with unloving adoptive parents in an ex-council house on the edge of a drab commuter town. And they were *especially* not ordinary to somebody who'd lived on the streets. Ordinary to Jack, they were just Mum and Dad, but how could they ever be ordinary to *him?*

Rory had carried out his research, and his stomach had fallen as his anxiety had climbed. The De Lacys were influential. Philanthropists and benefactors, they were friends with the great and the good of the land. Or at least the rich and powerful, but Rory wasn't sure if that made them either great or good. Jack had seen his nerves, had read his rampaging thoughts, and had calmed and reassured him. The calming and reassuring had more often than not taken the form of them getting naked, hot and sweaty, and it had certainly taken Rory's nerves away. Just as it had that morning, before they'd loaded up the car, locked up the flat, and headed west. But that had been earlier and a million years ago.

They'd long since left the motorway and the larger main roads behind them. The four-wheeled drive twisted and turned down small winding country lanes. They passed the occasional car, but they were few and far between as they climbed higher and higher into the Devonshire hills. Spring was late this year, but a sudden burst of warmth and sunshine had woken up the earth, dousing everywhere with brilliant colour as flowers and shrubs blossomed, bright and vibrant against the deep rusty, red soil and the emerald-green grass.

"It's beautiful." Rory stared out of the window, entranced by the rich landscape. The lush green hills gave way to the rough heathland of the Dartmoor National Park. Huge outcrops of grey, ragged rocks reached up into the clear blue sky. Rory narrowed his eyes, watching what looked like ants crawling over one.

"Rock climbers and abseilers," Jack said, following Rory's gaze. "This area's a mecca for it. Never quite understood the appeal, but my sister Caroline's keen.

Shit!" He slammed on the breaks, sending both of them lurching forward.

Filling the windscreen was a tan, hairy face, rubbery lips moving over huge tombstone teeth, as a ragged mane lifted and fell in the breeze. The stocky Dartmoor pony gave them a look of disdain before ambling away to take up a place next to a roadside boulder and applied itself to chomping on the sparse, rough gorse.

"They're everywhere." Rory looked out at the famous wild moorland ponies, which he'd only ever seen on TV, tough and rugged like the land they lived on. As well as ponies, sheep with ragged, matted wool dotted the moor, every one of them munching on the sparse offering of grass. Rory opened the window and was blasted by the smell of – shit. "Aw." He wrinkled his nose and brought the window up. "Is that the famous country smell?"

Jack laughed. "Sure is. If you've been brought up breathing in car fumes, country aromas are a bit of a shock to the system. You'll get used to it."

"Are they really wild, or do they go somewhere at night, for shelter?"

"Yes, they are wild, and no, they don't get herded up at night. And if you're wondering whether you can pet them, the answer's no – and especially at this time of year when there will be young roaming around. The adults are protective and so are liable to become aggressive if anybody gets too close. Come on, not long now." Jack put the car into gear, and they moved off.

*The adults are protective and so are liable to become aggressive if anybody gets too close. . .* With his first encounter with Jack's parents looming, Rory hoped those words didn't apply to the human population as he hunkered down in his seat and watched the bleak and beautiful countryside unroll before him.

*Bloody hell.*

Rory swallowed down the dry, hard lump that lodged in his throat as Jack steered the car through the open wrought-iron gates. They crunched their way along the gravel drive, towards the distant house through an avenue of tall, stately trees. Rory had no idea what trees they were, but they were old and established.

*Just like the De Lacy family.*

Seeing photos of the house and online was one thing, but looming up ahead of him, solid, grand, and imposing was something else altogether. The soft grey stone house – if it could even be called that – was like somewhere you'd visit on a Sunday afternoon, finishing up in the tea rooms after poking around the souvenir shop and coming away with a De Lacy-themed tea towel. Rory clenched his lower lip between his teeth, willing himself not to explode with hysterical, nervous laughter.

The car drew up at the bottom of a wide set of steps, bracketed on each side with a stone pillar featuring a mythical creature clutching the family coat of arms. A woman emerged through the open wooden double doors and made her steady way down, a Golden Labrador bouncing at her heels. Rory hadn't even got out of the car, and he wanted to run away. He stole a glance at Jack, who was smiling at the woman who stood waiting on the bottom step.

*Too late to turn back. . .*

"Here we are. The Manor House. Come and meet my mum."

## CHAPTER TWO

"Jack, darling. Give me a big hug – Badger, down." Diana glowered at the overexcited young dog jumping around at her feet. Badger whined as he did as he was told, but Diana's stern reprimand didn't stop his tail from swishing from side to side in greeting.

Jack gave himself up to his mum's all-embracing hug that squeezed the breath from his lungs. Diana was petite and soft-looking in her signature cashmere, but under the fluffy outer layer, she was a woman of steel.

"Hi, Mum. I'd rather all my ribs were left intact."

"Nonsense! You do exaggerate." All but shoving Jack aside, Diana focused her attention on Rory hanging back between Jack and the car.

*This is it...* Jack held his breath.

"Hello, Lady De Lacy." He offered his hand, which Diana squeezed in a firm, short handshake.

"Rory. I'm so happy to meet you at last. And please, call me Diana. I'm sure Jack could have brought you down before now," she said, narrowing her eyes at Jack in accusation, "but you're here now, and that's all that matters. Come along inside."

Diana started to hustle them toward the steps leading up to the heavy, dark doors, their footsteps crunching on the deep gravel drive.

"Thank you. We'll just get our luggage—"

"Fred will bring it in," she said, waving a hand towards the car. "Ah, here he is."

A burly, balding man with the ruddy face and muscles of somebody who'd spent a lot of his life in the outdoors, rounded the corner of the house and strode towards them. Jack greeted him with a grin as he threw Fred the car keys, which he caught with ease.

"Fred'll park the car in one of the garages around the back of the house, then bring our bags up," Jack said as he caught Rory's questioning eyes.

It was what Fred did and had always done for as long as Jack could remember. Within minutes of arriving back at the home he'd been born and brought up in, Jack was already slipping back into a way of life that was as alien to the one he lived back in London as creatures from Mars or the dark side of the moon. He glanced at Rory, being ushered into the house. *Oh God, I've got so much to explain...*

Inside the cavernous hall, Jack breathed a relieved sigh as his mother led them towards the Morning Room.

As he'd pulled up, the thought had gripped him that Rory's first introduction to the house would be the King's Parlour. It had been generations since the De Lacys had received visits from royalty, but the grandest, and for Jack the least liked room in the manor, was where special guests were received, and as far as Jack was concerned, there was nobody more special than Rory.

Bright, comfortable, and welcoming, the Morning Room was the heart of the house, of the home, and of the De Lacy family. It was the inner sanctum, and few were granted admittance. Jack pushed the fingers of one hand through his fair hair, trying to ignore their shaking. Everything was going to be fine. . . but one look at Rory's ramrod straight back and stiff, tense shoulders told him that, at the moment, *everything* was too much.

"Mum, hold on a moment."

Diana stopped and turned to Jack, her brows lifted in a silent question.

"We've had a long journey. Give us a bit of time to get ourselves sorted out, okay?"

"Of course you have, darling," she said after a tiny hesitation. "What was I thinking? I rarely drive to

London anymore, so I forget how tiresome the journey is. I'm sorry," she said, shifting her gaze to Rory. "You must think I'm very thoughtless."

"No, not at all, but I wouldn't mind—"

"A chance to catch your breath. I quite understand. I'll see you both in the Morning Room when you're refreshed. Badger, come." A moment later she was gone, the young dog bounding at her side.

"Come on, let's get upstairs." Jack bundled Rory back down the way they'd come and up the sweeping staircase.

"So, you have a guy to carry luggage and park the car?" Rory said under his breath.

"Erm. . ." Yes, perhaps a little chat was in order.

~

"How far does your family's land go for?" Rory leaned against the window, looking out over the gardens to the open fields beyond.

"Just beyond that woodland." Jack came up behind Rory and slipped his arms around his waist.

Since they'd got together at Christmas, Jack had answered every question Rory had asked about his family. He'd shown Rory photos of his parents and older brother and sister, of the house, the village of Polton Lacy, which his family owned most of and had lent part of its name to, and of the surrounding countryside. He'd not attempted to hide anything, but only now was Jack truly starting to understand that hearing about the De Lacys or reading about them or seeing them online wasn't the same as experiencing them. Even if so far it had only been his mother.

"Ah, okay. Well, that woodland is miles away, and I'm not going to ask how far *just beyond* really means. Your mum seems. . ."

"Intimidating?"

"I was going to say a bit scary, but I guess it's the same thing, really." Rory twisted around in Jack's arms.

"I don't want any of this." Jack released one arm from around Rory's waist and with the fingers of his free hand rubbed tiny circles over Rory's puckered brow. "No frowns, no worry lines, okay? I don't want that lovely—sweet—face—of yours to end up—looking like—a prune." Jack punctuated his words with little kisses, on Rory's brow, his nose and, finally, his lips.

"A prune? You think I look like a prune?"

"I like prunes, but I don't want my boyfriend to look like one. That's better." Jack swept aside Rory's glossy dark hair, which had flopped back over his brow.

Jack's heart flipped in a perfect somersault when Rory's lips lifted in a warm, soft smile. *But doesn't it always, every time he looks at me?*

"Come and sit down," he said, easing Rory over to the bed.

Jack could feel Rory's nerves coursing through him. He wanted his boyfriend to get to know his family and feel at ease, but he'd only do that if he could just be not so scared.

"I know that coming here, to all this, is a bit strange." Jack waved an arm in the general direction of the window as Rory's eyebrows shot up and disappeared into his hairline.

"A *bit* strange?"

"Okay, really, totally, one hundred per cent weird. But my family aren't a bunch of snobs who'll look down on you. I know that's what you're thinking, but it's just not true. They're not like that. They value people for who they are, not what school they went to, or—"

Rory huffed. "Just as well, as I don't think Fuzzy Hill Boys' School will be winning prizes for academic excellence any time soon."

"Fuzzy Hill? You went to a school called Fuzzy Hill?" Jack began to laugh.

Rory shrugged and tried to look offended, but soon he was joining in.

*That's better.*

The gentle banter between them, the playfulness, that's who they were, and that was who Jack wanted

Rory to be for the next few days, as natural and at ease with his family as Rory was with him.

Rory's shoulders relaxed, and the worry lines that still ghosted his brow began to fade. They didn't disappear completely, but at least Rory no longer looked as if he was afraid he was about to be eaten alive, and Jack counted that as a win.

"Seriously though," Jack said, enfolding Rory's hands in his own. "My family want to get to know you because they know how happy you've made me."

"Have I? Really? It's only been a few months—"

"And they've been the best of my life. Never doubt that, and never doubt that we've got months and years ahead of us to be even happier. Look, I might not get to see as much of my family as I'd like, with them here most of the time and me in London, but they mean the world to me, and I want them to mean the world to you too. And they will, if you give them a chance. Will you?"

Rory's head bowed. "I'm sorry. I never wanted you to think I didn't want to get to know them. I do." Rory looked up, determination shining from his chestnut-brown eyes.

Scared to death but defiant, determined to do the right thing. This was the man Jack had fallen in love with and loved more with every passing day.

"But only if you promise me they won't laugh and

point when I try to butter my bread with the fish knife or mistake the finger bowl for the soup course." Laughter danced in Rory's eyes and tugged at his lips.

"Oh, no, they wouldn't do that," Jack said, his face deadpan. "The nouveaux riches would, but not my family. The De Lacys are old money and have class, so they'd pretend not to notice. Anyway, you can get away with anything as long as you treat the dogs well and feed them titbits from the dinner table. Come on," Jack said, his face dissolving into smiles. "Mum's waiting to give you a grilling over tea and cake. But don't worry, because I'll stop you from getting too burnt."

*I hope.*

## CHAPTER THREE

"If he becomes a bore, just shove him aside. I mean Badger, not Jack." Diana snorted as she cut another slice of cake and landed it on Rory's plate. It was the third piece, not forgetting the huge cream-and-jam-laden scone she'd insisted Rory take. This is Devonshire after all, she'd said. The home of the cream tea.

"No, that's okay." Rory smiled down at Badger and tickled him behind the ear. Badger's tail thumped, and his long pink tongue lolled over the side of his open jaw.

Jack could have sworn Badger smiled back as he stared up at Rory with adoring eyes as chocolate brown as Rory's own. The young Golden Lab had fallen in love with Rory as much as Rory had fallen in love with him. And thank God for that, Jack thought. If there was one way to win over his mum, it was by winning over the dogs.

"I wouldn't shove him away. I'd just tell him to go and lie in the corner and not be a nuisance. Jack, I mean. Not Badger."

Diana's laughter burst the brief bubble of silence.

"You've got him house-trained. Good, because that's exactly what he needs."

Jack's head snapped between his boyfriend and his mum.

"It's good to know I'm thought of as highly as the dog," Jack said as he reached for his tea.

"Oh, no, darling. You haven't reached that dizzy height. Or not yet." Diana leaned over the coffee table and patted Jack's hand.

The cake in Jack's stomach began to feel a little less like concrete. Okay, it had just been chit-chat for the last half hour, and most of that had been about Badger and the various other dogs the family owned, but it had helped to settle some of Rory's nerves too if the colour that had returned to his cheeks and the loose way he crossed his feet at his ankles was anything to go by. They were small signs and would be missed by anybody else, but in the few short months since they'd been in each other's lives, Jack was already becoming an expert in reading his boyfriend's moods and thoughts. Jack sunk a little lower into the squashy sofa, the hard muscles in his back and shoulders softening a tiny bit more.

"I'm sorry Roger isn't here. He has business to see to in Bristol, and then he has to stay to attend a formal dinner. He'll be back tomorrow, around supper time. Now." Diana clapped her hands together and focused every scrap of her attention on Rory. "You must tell me about yourself. Jack says you're a chef, so I hope this meets with your approval." Diana indicated the cake-laden coffee table.

"It certainly does. Perhaps I could have the recipe for the carrot cake? It's the best I've had."

Jack continued to nibble at his slice, tamping down the smile aching to break out over his face. The spread of cakes had been baked by Anne, who'd been the family's housekeeper-cook for longer than he'd been alive. Without knowing it, by praising Anne's baking and making a friend of Badger, Rory was shinning his way up the pole of his mother's approval. Or maybe he *had* realised. Rory deserved a reward for being a smart boy. A very special reward, later, when they were alone in their bedroom. Jack shifted in the squashy sofa.

"Yes, I trained as a chef, so I've worked in restaurants, but I'm working in an artisan bakery near to our – er, Jack's – flat."

"Our flat," Jack corrected, taking Rory's hand in his and giving it a squeeze.

*And it* is *our flat.* Rory had made the place feel more like a home than it ever had, and he needed to be recognised for that. He glanced over at Diana, her expression calm, her lips lifted with a friendly smile that told Jack nothing about what she was thinking.

"So you're the head baker?"

"No. I'm not even the assistant. I did persuade the owner to make a couple of changes to the usual line, as an experiment, which went down well."

"So what is it you do, if not bake?"

"Well, they've just opened up a café area. I serve behind the counter, mainly. Help to clean up, that kind of thing."

"It suits both of us," Jack said, looking from Rory's reddening face to Diana. "Restaurant hours are punishing and anti-social."

"Yes, I imagine they are. Ah, this tea's gone cold. I'll call Anne for a fresh pot."

"Are you okay?" Jack whispered when Diana got up and went to the house phone in the corner of the room, connecting her to the kitchen.

"I think so, but—"

Diana came back and sat down. "You really have made a friend for life." Diana nodded to Badger, who slapped a furry, clumsy paw on Rory's knee and stared up at him with pleading, pitiful cocoa-brown eyes.

"He's lovely, but I'm sure he only wants to be my

friend because of the scrap of cake I gave him." Rory scrubbed Badger behind his floppy ear.

"Have you ever kept dogs?"

"Kept dogs? Er, well, my parents, or adoptive parents I should say, they had a mutt—erm, chihuahua mix of some kind, I mean. It wasn't the friendliest of dogs, not like this boy. They only had it for a few months before they took it back to the rescue centre. They got a hamster after that."

*A chihuahua mix.* Jack knew exactly what his mother would think of that. Dogs, in her eyes, came in one kind only: gun dogs. Labradors, spaniels, retrievers. Not chihuahua mixes.

"I still don't know how you met," Diana said, her face as calm as the village pond as she looked from one to the other.

Jack's stomach tightened.

They'd talked about this, over and over, about how they were going to answer the question they both knew they'd be asked. Well, that question was being asked now. Over good, if not the best, family china and silverware. There was nothing shameful about how he'd found the best thing in his life bundled up on his doorstep, but faced with the stark question. . . Next to him, Jack felt Rory stiffen and go still, and Badger whined when Rory's fingers went quiet in the dog's golden fur.

"Lady Diana?" The rattle of china on a tray had them all looking towards the door as Anne came in, taking slow and steady steps across the faded Turkish carpet.

"Thank you, Anne. Let me take that." Diana took the tray from the elderly woman.

Jack gave Anne a warm smile, and she replied with one as welcoming as his own. He'd call into the kitchen later to give the housekeeper the big hug she deserved. For now, all his attention was focused on his scared-to-death boyfriend, who sat next to him, as still and rigid as a statue.

Rory's eyes were huge in his blanched face, and he'd edged forward on the sofa. The pose was a stark reminder of the night they'd met, when he'd taken the freezing cold, desperate man not just into his home but into his heart. That night, too, Rory had perched on the edge of his seat, tense, full of nerves, and ready to flee.

*Let me handle this*, was Jack's unspoken message when Rory turned to him.

"I found Rory sitting on my doorstep. He was in a bit of a fix, and I was in a position to help."

"Sitting on Jack's doorstep? I don't quite understand. What was this fix you were in? How was Jack able to help, exactly?" Diana raised a perfect brow as she handed Rory fresh tea, but Rory's hands shook so much he sloshed much of it into the saucer.

"I—"

Jack took them from him and clunked them down on the table.

"This isn't an interview, Mum. Nor an interrogation. The main thing is, we met, and that's all that matters."

The question they both knew would be asked, and it was already going wrong. This was not how telling his family that Rory had been living on the streets was supposed to go. He'd always told Rory his mother – both his parents – were open and non-judgemental, but everything in his mother's tone told Jack that she was ready to judge Rory. *Thanks, Mum. Thanks a fucking million.*

Jack glared at Diana over the tea and cake. A slight flush crept up her cheeks, and she brushed her palms over her soft grey cashmere skirt in a rare show of discomfort.

"Of course it isn't. And Jack is correct. The fact that you met is really all that matters. You'll have to excuse me, now, I'm afraid," she said, standing up, her composure back in place. "I've some estate business I need to deal with. Supper is at seven o'clock, and you'll get an opportunity to meet my daughter Caroline and the Monsters."

"The Monsters?" Rory said.

"My grandsons. They're actually very sweet, but I couldn't possibly tell them that."

A moment later, she was gone.

"Bloody hell." Rory flopped back against Jack, as though the wire holding him up had been cut. "That was—"

"I'm so sorry, Ro," Jack said. "She's to the point, but you're right, that was—"

"Your mum wanting to know about what you've dragged home."

Jack's blood froze. *Dragged home?* Jack sat up and twisted Rory around to face him.

"Don't talk like that. You're my partner, which means you've got every right to feel comfortable being here."

"She wants to know who I am. Don't blame her for it."

"You're taking her side?"

"No, it's not about taking sides. Maybe we should have told her and your dad about how we met before we came down. Perhaps it would have got the first hurdle out of the way. Who knows? Don't forget, only a handful of months ago you were telling everybody about your new boyfriend but were refusing to say anything more about him. No wonder she's eager to find out about me."

"Don't remind me about that." Jack shivered, and Rory smiled.

It seemed like a dim and distant memory. In order to save face after his long-term boyfriend dumped him, Jack had boasted about the hot new man in his life – a hot new man who hadn't existed until he'd persuaded the waif and stray he'd found sheltering on his doorstep to play the part of his boyfriend for Christmas. It hadn't taken more than a breath to realise that the fake love they were showing to the world was turning into something real.

"Anyway, you've probably frightened her off from asking anything more."

Jack huffed out a laugh. "You really think so?" His mother didn't know the meaning of the word frightened.

Rory smiled, but it didn't reach his eyes, and Jack's stomach tightened as he wondered what the coming days would bring.

*If we can last that long.*

## CHAPTER FOUR

Soon after Diana left, they escaped the Morning Room.

Jack led Rory to the herb garden at the back of the house, enclosed within redbrick walls stained and pitted with age. Hardy herbs that had withstood the winter were lined up with those that were just beginning to wake and greet the warmer spring days.

"This is magical," Rory said, breathing in deep the scents wafting on the breeze.

The pungent aroma of rosemary and sage filled the warm air, reminding him of the kitchens he'd worked in. The soft leaves of some of the more delicate herbs were yet to make a show, but bright flowers on various shrubs Rory didn't know the names of had opened themselves up to the bees that buzzed around them. It seemed too early in the year for bees, but maybe, Rory thought, spring with all its new life and promise came earlier to the rich and verdant West Country.

Jack nodded. "It's where I liked playing most of all when I was a kid and getting under the feet of the gardeners until I was reprimanded by my parents and ordered away."

Rory glanced over at Jack and relief loosed the rope binding his chest. Jack's lips curved up in a smile, the happy memories smoothing the tense lines that had settled over his face since the awkward encounter with Diana.

"Come on, let's take a walk around the box garden."

"The what?" Rory asked, but Jack just smiled.

Rory let Jack take his hand and lead him out through a low, narrow wooden door into a formal garden laid out along geometric lines. It was as different to the random, almost wild feel of the herb garden as it was possible to get but as stunning in its own straight-lined, rigid way.

"Why's it called the box garden?"

"It's got something to do with the way it's been planted. Lots of square boxes of flowers surrounded by low hedges boxing them in."

*It's like visiting a stately home. Maybe Diana will ask me to cough up a tenner later on.* "Do you open to the public?" Rory blurted out.

"Only on four days a year and just the grounds. Mum leads a short tour. It's actually rather well known because it's one of the best examples of formal garden landscaping in a private house. She grumbles about doing it, but I think she secretly enjoys showing it off, as well as providing cream teas in a marquee."

Rory tried to imagine Diana dispensing tea and scones, with an apron tied around her middle to protect all that expensive cashmere.

"It's best seen from above," Jack said, climbing a set of stone steps leading up to a wide veranda. They leaned on its low, stone wall and looked out.

It was as far from what had laughingly been called a garden at the home Rory had grown up in with the Kincaids as it was possible to get. *That* had been nothing more than a scrubby patch of grass, some weed-choked borders, and a collection of potted plants, wilting for lack of care and attention.

"It's beautiful, like a well-kept park," Rory said as he followed Jack's gaze.

Beyond the box garden, a rich green lawn, as perfect and pristine as a bowling green, fell away towards what Jack called The Pond. It looked more like a lake to Rory. An ornamental bridge, in the same grey stone as the wall they both leaned on, spanned The Pond about halfway across. Beyond and past a small copse, the land rose to a hill behind which, Jack said, was the village of Polton Lacy. On top of the hill was a tower, a dark and imposing silhouette against the soft blue sky. The Tor, Jack called it as he pointed it out, a folly put up by one of his ancestors when romantic ruins were all the rage and a must-have for every wealthy, fashionable family.

"Are you okay? Really?" Jack turned and pulled Rory into his chest, and Rory sighed as he was enveloped in Jack's warmth.

For a moment or two, Rory said nothing as he snuggled into Jack's body.

"I thought I'd be able to handle it, but now, I'm not so sure." Rory pushed away from the warm sanctuary of Jack's arms and looked up into his boyfriend's deep blue eyes. "What if they think I'm not good enough? What if they look at me and think that, in you, I've—I've seen a chance to do well for myself." *That I've found myself a meal ticket to grab hold of.*

The thought had wormed its way into him, growing bigger and fatter as the day got nearer and nearer for him to meet Jack's family. Jack's old, aristocratic, wealthy family. Wouldn't they have the right to be suspicious of the stranger who'd turned up with nothing and had almost straight away made a comfortable home with their much-loved son, who had the means to give him everything he wanted?

"Not good enough? You're the best thing that's ever

happened to me. You came into my life and turned it upside down, and thank God you did. Don't ever tell me or anybody that you're not good enough. But most of all, never tell yourself that. You understand?"

Jack's gaze pinned Rory to the spot. Rory nodded, his mouth too parched and his throat too constricted for him to speak.

"I know we said we'd be open and honest about telling them everything, but we don't have to say a word, not if you don't want to. It's you that matters in all this, not me and not my parents."

"No," Rory said, finding his voice. "I won't have you keeping secrets from them. That's not who you are. This isn't just about me; it's about us."

A breeze blew up, whipping around them. The sun had sunk lower in the sky as afternoon reached towards evening.

"Let's leave it for now. I think just getting here and surviving a first meeting with my mother's enough for one day, don't you? Come on, let's go in. It's getting too cold to hang around out here. I'll give you a tour of my room if you like?"

"A tour? I thought only the gardens were included in the ticket price. And I saw it earlier, remember?"

Jack grinned, and Rory laughed, relieved the mood had lightened.

"It's a private tour. And anyway, my room is best

viewed naked and from the bed. You get a much better appreciation from that angle."

Before Rory could say another word, Jack grabbed his hand and hauled him back towards the house. The very drafty house. A shiver of anticipation danced along Rory's spine. *I hope they've turned the central heating up a bit more...*

# CHAPTER FIVE

"Uncle Jack, Uncle Jack." Screams louder than a jet engine came from two boys with bright red hair hurling themselves across the room at breakneck speed.

"Monsters, behave." Diana didn't have to raise her voice to be commanding, but the two boys were on a trajectory that couldn't be stopped, and as one they cannonballed into Jack before they attempted to climb up him like two young mountain goats.

"Hello you two, come and give me a cuddle." Jack wrapped an arm around each, and the two children clung to him so hard it was as if they were attempting to burrow inside Jack's skin.

Jack was beaming. Hugging and kissing each boy in turn, the love and sheer joy at seeing his nephews shining bright in his big, soppy smile.

One boy peeked over at Rory and buried his head back into Jack's leg when Rory waved.

"Caroline, come and meet Rory," Diana said.

Rory's heart lurched. He pasted a smile on his face he hoped didn't make him look like a rabbit caught in the headlights, praying Jack's sister wasn't a Diana Mark II. He stood, pushing up from the stripy sofa, and the face he looked into could have been Jack in female form.

"Hello." Rory extended his hand for Caroline to shake, but she batted it away and enveloped him in a hug. His nose twitched from the faint citrus perfume she wore, a softer version of Jack's cologne.

"I'm so glad you're here, Rory, I truly am."

Caroline stepped back and looked at him through eyes as warm and friendly as her smile. Rory's racing heart began to calm, and the tension softened in his shoulders as he returned her smile.

"It's such a shame my husband, Tim, isn't here to meet you. He's away on business at the moment, but if you come back in the summer – which I hope you do – you'll also get to meet George, who's mine and Jack's elder brother. He's currently working in Dubai. It's intolerable in the summer, he always says." Caroline squeezed Rory's hand. "Oh, goodness." She looked at Jack and shook her head, but the smile never left her lips. "He lets them walk all over him. Literally."

Rory followed her gaze and grinned. Jack was on his hands and knees, both boys riding on his back, laughing and giggling as Jack shook his head and made whinnying sounds like a horse.

"Monsters, dismount." Diana's imperious, crystal clear voice finally had its effect. The first flush of their excitement over, the boys tumbled from Jack's back and ran into the waiting arms of their grandmother.

"Hugo and Henry." Caroline nodded to her sons. "But generally known as the Monsters and for good reason. She pretends to be strict with them, but they have her around their little fingers," Caroline whispered. "And it gives me a break, which is always welcome. Hey, little brother."

Jack came across and caught his sister in a bear hug, lifting her up from the floor.

Brother and sister grinned at each other when Jack put Caroline down, amid her laughter and mock chiding. The likeness between the two was startling, but it couldn't outshine the love and affection they had for one another. Love and affection, in the bosom of his family, Jack had what Rory had never experienced but had always craved.

As Jack and Caroline caught up with each other, Rory's mind drifted away from the yellow-and-white-striped room and back to a cramped, bland living room where the TV was always switched on and blaring something mindless from the corner. The Kincaid family, squashed together in a house that wasn't much bigger than the Morning Room and from where his adoptive parents waged a constant battle to keep his spoiled, out-of-control twin sisters in some kind of order. Sisters who weren't really his sisters, and whose birth had ousted Rory from Peter and Sonia's tepid affections. Rory had tried to love the girls, had tried his best to be their big brother, but almost from the time they could talk, they'd told him he wasn't their brother, they wished he wasn't there, and that he'd been a mistake. *Out of the mouths of babes...*

They hadn't known what they were saying. They'd just been repeating the words of their parents. His place in the home of a family that had ceased to be his, if it ever had been, had been spat out at him by two children who really were no better than monsters. Rory had taken the first way out he could find, a way out that had ended up plunging him into the depths of despair but which had ultimately brought him to Jack. Maybe he had something to thank the Kincaids for after all.

"What? Sorry?" Rory blinked as he looked from Jack to Caroline and back again.

Caroline laughed, the slight backwards throw of her head and rich, throaty chuckle so like Jack's you'd have thought brother and sister were twins rather than separated in age by almost ten years.

"You were miles away," she said. "I was saying that you've certainly shoved little brother here out of the funk he'd fallen into after that beastly situation with Sam."

"Oh, erm. . ." Rory turned to Jack, whose face was as red as Rory's felt.

"Well, Sam's history. He's gone and good riddance." Jack draped his arm around Rory's shoulders and squeezed tight.

"Good to hear it." Caroline grinned, a wicked glint in her eye. "Because the new boyfriend's an improvement on the last."

Jack felt for Rory's hand under the table, kneading Rory's cold fingers.

They'd all trooped off to the kitchen, where Anne had laid out a selection of meats and cheeses, warm oven-fresh breads, olives, and salads. A bottle of chilled white wine and a jug of water accompanied the food.

*This is more like it.*

Gathered around the old, scarred table, the kitchen shared the honour with the Morning Room for being the heart of the house. The kitchen was warm, and the food good and plentiful. Jack pulled another bottle of wine from the fridge and topped up everybody's glass. Relaxed and informal, this was the side of his family Jack wanted Rory to experience. Earlier had been a hiccup, a hitch, a blip.

As Diana and Caroline exchanged news about the village, explaining to Rory who was who and peppered with irreverent comments from Caroline and arch, pithy observations from Diana, Rory was soon laughing. Jack's shoulders relaxed, the tension that had held them tight at last draining away.

The two boys, who'd spent more time feeding Badger than themselves, jumped down from the table as soon as Diana gave them a sharp nod. They threw themselves at the young dog, and the three of them were soon rolling around in furry knot.

"I hope you've left room for pudding, Rory." Diana peered at his empty plate.

Under the table Jack rubbed Rory's hand, trying to relay the telepathic message that the way to Diana's heart was to love the dogs and Anne's cooking.

"I—"

"Why's Uncle Jack holding Gory's hand?"

The shout from under the table was accompanied by a woof and a wet, raspy tongue laving over the back of Jack's hand.

"Because *Rory* is Uncle Jack's special friend,"

Caroline said, abandoning the plate she was dishing up from for a moment, and hauling Hugo, Henry and Badger out from under the table.

Jack turned to Rory, whose face was as red as the strawberries strewn all over the pavlova Caroline was dishing up.

"Your mum's right, *Gory* is my special friend. Very special indeed."

"Pudding!" The two boys squealed in unison, and Jack sighed with relief that the prospect of the sweet confection of meringue, sugar-steeped strawberries, and cream had swept away a barrage of awkward questions.

*We've had enough of those for one day.*

"Sorry about that," Caroline whispered to Rory, pushing a plate of pavlova towards him.

"Monsters, you can have pudding later." Diana glowered at her grandsons.

Hugo and Henry gave a combined moan, but Jack's promise they could have ice cream as well was enough to placate them as he shoved the bundle of boys and fur away.

The boys and dog tumbled around in the corner, leaving everybody else to tuck into the sweet and slightly chewy meringue, which was the perfect foil for the sharp berries and rich double cream piled on top.

"This is delicious. I've never eaten a pav this good before."

Jack grinned. *You're learning.*

The kitchen fell into silence as they dug into the dessert.

"Judith Henderson has had to pull out of the Best Bake in Show," Diana said with a barely concealed *harrumph.* "If we ask for late entrants, we'll be swamped, and that really would be too bothersome to sort."

It took Jack a moment to catch up with what his mother was talking about. Of course, the village fete, held each year on the Saturday before Easter Day. But who the hell was Judith Henderson?

"Who—?" Jack asked.

"Judith Henderson, formally Smith. Goodness, Jack, you must remember her. The youngest daughter of Smith's Family Butchers. She worked behind the counter before she had her children. Delightful young woman, but with the most ghastly acne. It could be most off-putting."

"Acne?" Jack tried to remember a spotty-faced but delightful young woman, presiding over Smith's Family Butchers display of steaks, chops, and sausages, but drew a blank.

"It's improved with age and a stronger ointment. But that's beside the point."

"Hmm, maybe I should become vegetarian," Caroline sniggered, earning herself a reprimanding glare from Diana.

"Perhaps Rory would like to enter the competition."

"Mum!" Jack put his spoon and fork down with a clatter. Where the hell had *that* idea come from? "We're not here – *Rory's* not here – to make cakes. You'll have to make do with one less entrant or open it up for late submissions."

"And be deluged with applications from amateur bakers who think they're auditioning for The Great British Bake-Off?" Caroline chimed in. "Honestly, Jack, I thought the politics around selecting entrants for Biggest Leek in Show was bad enough, but that's nothing compared to Best Bake. All these baking programmes on the television have turned it into warfare. Last year there was even a rumour one of the entrants had her bundt tampered with."

"Well, I hope she saw a doctor about it," Jack grumbled. "Sorry, but no. Bundt tampering or sponge fiddling isn't our problem."

"It would certainly get us out of a fix. Perhaps it should be Rory's decision." Diana turned to Rory.

"No." Jack glared at his mother.

First her clumsy questioning and now pressurising Rory into donning an apron and wielding a cake tin.

He'd told Rory his family were easy-going, even casual. Maybe his version of that wasn't everybody else's. He'd been away too long, and it was beginning to show.

Jack looked at Rory, sure he'd see a silent plea for help, but instead of horror at Diana's outrageous suggestion, there was a dawning interest shining in his eyes.

"If it helps. . ."

"Excellent!" Diana and Caroline chimed in unison.

"Really? Do you *really* want to do this? I mean, you work in the bakery all week—"

"But I don't get to bake. There's no room for another baker at Arturo's. That's been made very clear. And this kitchen is a bit bigger than yours."

Rory smiled. Big, bright, and wide, it was the first genuine smile Jack had seen light up Rory's face since they'd arrived. Rory wanted to do this, he really did, and there he was, about to do his best to wipe that smile away.

"Are you sure it'd be okay?" Rory looked between Diana and Caroline. "I mean, isn't the competition just meant for local people?"

"Not technically. To be honest, a healthy injection of new blood would be welcome," Diana said.

"Just not in the actual cake. The head of the Polton Lacy Ladies' Guild would have a fit," Caroline added with a wink. "You'd be doing us a huge favour, Rory. We need somebody to come in and give the Grannies' Army a run for their money."

"Caroline, really." Diana's attempt at a prim reprimand fell apart when her lips quirked. "That's agreed, then. Rory is the official late entrant for Best Bake in Show. Now, shall we take coffee in the Morning Room?"

~

"You don't have to do it, you know. I don't want you to feel you have to go along with it. Mum expects everybody to fall in with her plans, but you're not obliged to. I won't have you being pressurised, Ro."

"She's not pressurising me into anything." Rory pushed himself up on one elbow and looked down at Jack. "I want to do it. It'd make me feel like I'm a bit more part of all this."

"All this?" Jack said, reaching up and pushing a stray lock of raven-black hair out of Rory's chestnut-brown eyes.

"You know what I mean. I never, ever thought I'd be with a posh bloke whose family live in a castle."

"It's not a castle."

"Okay, but neither is it an ex-council house."

"No, and I suppose it's a touch bigger than the average," Jack said with a twist of his lips, "but mainly it's a family home, even if the family who live in it are on the posh side."

"So you admit you're a posh bloke?"

"Maybe just a little bit."

Rory flopped down onto his back, next to Jack on the bed where they both lay.

When Caroline had gathered up her sons to return to her home in the village, Jack had told his mother they'd had a long day and were going to have an early night. With the fire in the grate burning low, the bedroom was warm and snuggly against the chilly spring evening.

Jack gathered Rory up in his arms, his body sighing as Rory pressed close. He kissed the top of Rory's head, the soft strands of his boyfriend's hair silky against his lips. Boyfriend? No, Rory was so much more than that. Even the more formal *partner* didn't come close. Jack closed his eyes. *If Rory had stumbled into some other doorway. . . If I hadn't have asked him in. . . If it hadn't have been snowing. . .* So many *ifs*. God alone knew where both of them would have been *if*. . . Jack wound his arms tighter around the beautiful, warm man who filled his heart to overflowing.

"Don't let everything overwhelm you. Mum can be hard to stand up to, and I don't want you to feel you have to say yes in order to win her approval." Jack held his breath as Rory wriggled out of his arms and looked at him. Rory's face was serious, all trace of his bright and sunny smile gone. Jack's chest tightened. "Rory, I didn't—"

"Shush, and just listen to me." Rory pressed his forefinger against Jack's lips, his dark eyes focused and solemn. "I didn't agree because I felt pressured, whatever you think. I agreed because I want to do it. Baking is a world I feel comfortable and confident in. That's how I want to feel all the time I'm here. When we tell your parents about us, I want to be able to look them in the eye, and I won't be able to do that if I feel I can't meet them on equal terms. I know it sounds stupid, but being able to prove myself with something I know I'm good at will help me do that. It's not about trying to get into your mum's good books, Jack."

"You don't have to prove yourself to anybody. Coming here was never meant to be an ordeal you had to endure or a test you had to pass," Jack said, easing Rory's finger from his lips. "If that's how being here makes you feel, we don't have to stay. We can go back to London."

"But I do have to prove myself, whatever you might think. My background is so different, and I *am* overwhelmed by it all because how can I not be? I mean, meeting your parents was always going to be nerve-wracking enough, without everything else. But I won't run away because of a stumble at the first hurdle. Being here, being part of what you love so much is important to me because it's important to you." Rory reached up and drew the backs of his fingers over Jack's stubbled jawline, sending a tingling warmth all the way to Jack's groin.

Realisation hit Jack hard in the chest. Rory wanted to feel as if he had some control, some say over things. Yes, Jack knew the world he'd grown up in was as far from Rory's as it was possible to get, but all he'd done was bat that aside. *My family's great. They'll love you as much as you'll love them.* He'd said it over and over, believing every word. But it had been too simplistic. His love for his family and for Rory had fogged his vision, and it had been Rory who'd been clear-sighted despite his crippling nerves. The worlds they'd come from were poles apart, and he'd been a fool to try and ignore it. Rory didn't just need a map; he needed a strategy, even weapons, to navigate his way across an unknown landscape, and if stepping into the breach and going for Best Bake in Show gave him what he needed, then who was he to stand in his way? Saying yes to Diana had nothing to do with baking a cake; it was about survival.

Jack pushed Rory onto his back.

"You do know you're going to be going into battle, don't you?"

"Battle?"

"Oh yes." Jack shifted, his lips a moment from Rory's. "You'll be up against the post mistress and her Victoria sponge. The old bat's won three years in a row, and she'll be fighting to the death to retain the crown. And there's the vicar; he makes a mean fruit cake. When it comes to Best Bake you can forget all about Christian charity; that guy's out to win, and it's dog collars off. And let's not forget the ladies of the Women's Institute with their jam sponges, and deadly rivals of the Polton Lacy Ladies' Guild. I tell you, all those sweet old grannies are mean bitches beneath their smiles and blue rinses."

Rory's answering grin was wicked, all trace of nerves and worry gone. "Oh yeah," Rory murmured, his pavlova-sweet breath glancing over Jack's lips sending a delicious shiver all the way along Jack's spine. "They haven't had a taste of my muffins yet. Nor my lemon drizzle, and as for my treacle tart—"

"Ah fuck." Jack squeezed the words through gritted teeth as Rory rolled his hips forward, nudging at the bulge in the front of Jack's jeans. He needed something hot and sweet from Rory, all right, but it wasn't his man's treacle tart.

"Or my molten fondants, oozing melted chocolate and dripping in cream. You like that best of all, don't you, Jack?"

Jack groaned, then gasped as Rory in a surprise move flipped him onto his back before inching down his body, almost stopping his heart when Rory rubbed his cheek against the straining swelling pushing out against his jeans.

"Ro—*ahh.*" Jack shivered as the zip on his jeans was opened up. A moment later his cock was free of its soft cotton prison.

"Want to give me something oozy and dripping in cream?"

Jack's only answer was a strangled moan as Rory's damp breath wafted over his hot, pulsing shaft.

"I'll take that funny little noise as a yes, then, shall I?"

"You can—" It was as far as Jack got as Rory took him into his mouth.

## CHAPTER SIX

Rory yawned and stretched and thought about getting up. Instead he pushed himself further down under the duvet and snuggled against Jack, who snored softly. It was the only sound Rory could hear.

*It's so quiet.*

Rory couldn't hear a thing. No car doors slamming, no kids screaming, no ever-present low-level rumble of traffic. All the noises that were the backdrop to city life were absent in the deep countryside, and Rory lay listening to the silence, trying to decide if he liked it or not, before his stomach rumbled, issuing its morning demand for tea and toast.

He nudged Jack in the ribs and kicked his calf. All accidental of course, or so he'd claim when Jack woke up with a *what?* and a *where?* as he blinked at the world around him with unfocused eyes. But Jack didn't wake up and instead rolled onto his side as he muttered incomprehensible words before upping the tempo of his snores.

Rory sighed and slipped from the bed. Maybe by the time he'd had a shower and a shave, Jack would have woken up, so they could go down to breakfast together.

The shower cranked into life, pipework groaning and complaining at being brought into service so early, but the pressure was good and the water steaming hot. As the water pummelled down on him, Rory thought over the previous day.

There had been a stumble with Diana, but Caroline had literally welcomed him with open arms. And dinner, or supper as Diana had called it, had gone well on the whole. Scrubbing through his foamy hair, Rory's fingers slowed, then stopped.

The invitation to take part in the baking contest had felt like a thinly veiled order, but it had been a godsend. Rory wasn't sure if Jack had really understood when he'd told him that bringing some of his world into the De Lacy's was what he needed to help him stand tall. But why would Jack understand? The world that felt so alien to him was in Jack's blood, bones, and DNA. Jack may have lived a very different life in London, but upbringing and the weight of generations would never be easily wiped away.

Back in the bedroom, Jack was still sleeping, and Rory hesitated as he wondered whether or not to wake him. The clock on the bedside cabinet read 6.40 am. Back in London, they'd have both been up and ready to leave the flat, but Rory had to remind himself that they weren't in London. Far from it, he thought as he crossed to the window and looked out at the expanse of rich green grass and light blue sky. His stomach rumbled again, prompting Rory to quickly dress. Less than five minutes later, he was closing the bedroom door.

Outside, he paused, listening for any signs of life, but there was nothing except for the clanging of old pipework as the central heating system kicked in. Maybe everybody was still in bed. And who exactly *was* everybody? As far as he knew, there were only Diana, him, and Jack in the house. He swallowed hard and cast a look back at the closed door to his and Jack's room. As much as he wanted Jack to be with him, he wasn't going to wake him up. *I've woken you up and dragged you out of bed so that you can come with me to find some tea and toast* sounded limper than a bowlful of overcooked noodles.

Rory made his way down the oak staircase, under the grim and watchful painted eyes of long-dead De Lacys, every step he took creaking and cracking like a whip in the silent house. As he reached the bottom, the fast click of claws on flagstones greeted him as Badger bounded out of a shadowy corner and skidded to an ungainly stop at Rory's feet.

"Hello, boy." Rory bent forward to pat the tail-wagging bundle of golden fur. But Badger had other ideas as he rolled onto his back, legs flopping to the side and presenting a pink tummy. "Oh, you want a tickle, do you?"

Badger snorted as though saying *what do you think?*

"He's taken a shine to you, so you do realise that he'll try and stow away in the car when you go back to London?"

Rory jumped. He hadn't notice Diana come into the hallway. She wore a shabby long waxed coat that looked as if it had seen years' of wear, green wellington boots, and a brown woollen hat that reminded Rory of one he'd seen on a scarecrow on the edge of a field not far from the house. Rory knew he should have said good morning and made some witty comment about the dog, but his tongue was tied in a tight knot, and his throat had turned to stone as he stared up at Diana, feeling as stupid as he no doubt looked.

"I suppose you could eat some breakfast. I know I could." Diana's clear, crisp voice rang through the hallway.

"Erm, yes, please," Rory said, finding his voice at

last as he stood upright. At his feet, Badger whimpered for the attention he'd lost. "I was making my way to the kitchen, just to make a cup of tea. I hope you don't mind?"

"Of course not. Come along, I'm sure that we can cobble up a good country breakfast between us. You look like you need feeding up, if you'll excuse my saying so. Come," she said, turning on her heel and striding away.

Rory wasn't sure if she was speaking to him or Badger, but he jumped to attention and followed her retreating back into the depths of the house, claws clicking beside him on the flagstones as the dog followed too.

In the kitchen, Diana took off her coat and hat and slung them over a chair. Rory's eyes widened. In place of the elegant cashmere she'd worn the day before, Diana was dressed in old, baggy corduroys and a jumper that had more holes in it than a sieve.

"I like to take a walk around the estate each morning, or at least a part of it. If I'd have known you were an early riser, I'd have asked you to join me," Diana said over her shoulder.

"Jack showed me some of it yesterday. We had a walk around the herb and box gardens. They're stunning, but calling them gardens is a bit like calling a Sacher torte a chocolate muffin." The words tumbled from Rory without thought, and he cringed. What the hell had he just said? And where did the weird baking comparison come from?

Diana made a sound Rory supposed was meant to be a laugh as she pulled eggs, bacon, and sausages from the fridge.

"Your assessment is spot on. My thoughts ran along the same lines the first time I saw them. The gardens at the house I grew up in were far less formal. Make some tea, will you? Everything's on the side. This will be cooked soon."

Rory made tea, filling the pot that sat next to the kettle, as Diana began to dish out the fry-up.

"This looks and smells lovely. Thank you." His stomach rumbled in agreement, but Rory wondered how he was going to get through all the food heaped high on his plate.

"It is. We produce and butcher all our own meat, and we've won prizes at county shows."

Diana's words were matter-of-fact, as though home butchery was an everyday thing. But maybe it was, he thought, for families like the De Lacys. Rory had taken a basic butchery course at catering college, but it had made him feel sick.

Rory gave all his attention to his food, as much to appease his demanding stomach as it was not to make small talk. He had no idea what to say to somebody who could no doubt flit between appearing on the front cover of The Lady magazine as she could on Huntin', Shootin' & Fishin'. Was there such a magazine? Rory wondered. He had no idea, but he was sure that if there were, Diana would be a fully paid-up subscriber.

"Thank you, but I really can't eat any more. It was lovely, really good quality." *I'm gabbling.*

He picked up his tea and buried his face in his mug, his skin prickling under Diana's scrutiny of him from across the table. *Why didn't I wait for Jack to wake up?* But it was too late now, and he wasn't going to scurry away like a mouse, even if it was what he wanted to do.

"You're a guest in our home, Rory."

The words were bland and bald, a statement of fact. He *was* a guest, but Diana's words held a hint of something else. He didn't have long to discover what it was.

"You are, of course, at liberty to tell me to mind my own business, but I sensed I'd hit a very raw nerve yesterday, over tea. Jack's touchiness and dare I say it uncharacteristic flash of anger, though contained, is not like my son at all." Diana placed her mug down and gave Rory her full attention.

Rory's chest tightened as Diana's blue eyes bored into him.

"I ask not from idle curiosity, nor because I feel I

have some kind of parental right, but Jack's choices haven't always been the best, especially when they have concerned what might be called affairs of the heart. Jack's been hurt before, and I'm not just talking about that dreadful Sam. I won't stand by and see it happen again."

The delicious breakfast turned rancid in Rory's stomach. His lips were dry, his throat parched, and his tongue felt like thick, heavy leather in his mouth. Diana's eyes lasered into him, bright with the confidence and conviction that she had every right to say what she had.

She hadn't.

Rory sat rigid and straight in the chair, putting everything he had into his less than impressive five-feet-seven.

"Is that what you think I'm out to do?" Rory said, finding his voice that was little more than a croak.

"I don't know, Rory. That's what's at issue here. You came into Jack's life when he was at a low point, when he was vulnerable. He's a very loving and generous-hearted boy—"

"Jack's not a boy. He's a grown man and capable of making his own decisions about his life, even though you obviously don't think so."

A flash of satisfaction burned through Rory when

Diana's eyes opened wider and two red patches appeared on her cheeks.

*You didn't think I'd answer you back, did you?* Neither did he, but Diana's heavily hinted accusation that he had somehow latched on to a poor beaten and bruised Jack for his own ends crawled on his skin like flies over meat.

"Yes, he is a grown man, and I don't make a habit of intervening in his life – even though there have been times when I've been sorely tempted. Can you honestly blame me for being concerned? I'm Jack's mother and whether he's nine, twenty-nine, or fifty-nine, his happiness and welfare will always be of utmost importance to me."

"And you don't think I can make him happy or that his welfare isn't important to *me*? Is that what you're saying, Diana? Is it? Or are you really trying to say that I've found a good thing in Jack? Well, I *have* found a good thing but not in the way you think."

Rory clasped his hands together in an effort to stop them from shaking. Anger and indignation rose up in him on a fast rushing tide. He wanted to tell Diana to mind her own business and go to hell; he wanted to throw his chair back and stomp out of the kitchen; he wanted to pull Jack from the bed they'd shared so they could drive back to London; he wanted to do all of it, but more than that, he wanted to prove to Diana that she was *wrong*, and the only way to do that was to tell her the whole pitiful tale of how he and Jack had met. He would tell her who he was and who he had been, and he'd do it with his head held high.

*And she can take from it what she will, but she'll know the truth, and that's all that matters.*

"Jack saved my life. Without him, I'd be dead by now."

Diana reared back, her stony composure rocked for an instant.

"You think I'm exaggerating?" Rory glared at her, challenging her to contradict him.

"That's a bold statement. Had you been in an accident, were you—?"

"I was homeless." Rory cut off Diana. "I had nowhere to go, no food, and no money. I was surviving from day to day and got by from the odd handout from the rare passer-by who didn't walk past as though I were invisible. You talk about low points and being vulnerable. Well, I know exactly what they mean because I've lived them, and I only survived them because of Jack."

Rory and Diana stared at each other over the battered oak table. What would she think of his sorry tale? That he had not only survived but had beaten a dark and dangerous life with the aid of the good man who was her son? Or that he'd grabbed on to Jack's sincerely meant but misguided attempts to help and now had no intention of letting go? Rory didn't know, but as his head began to thrum with the tension that filled every inch of him, the one thing he *did* know was that he had to finish what he'd started. He inhaled a deep breath.

"I was sheltering in Jack's doorway, just before Christmas. All the hostels were full. It was snowing and freezing cold, and I wouldn't have made it through another night, let alone the rest of the winter. He could have kicked me out. It's what I expected him to do, but —but he didn't."

Had everything he'd said fallen on deaf ears? As he searched Diana's impassive, unreadable face, he had no idea. *She'll think what she wants to think.* The thought tasted bitter in his mouth. He rubbed his brow as though to rub away the headache that hammered in his skull.

"Jack is a good man." Diana paused as though weighing each word. "He was a good boy, he was a good teenager. He always did what was right." Diana shrugged. "Sometimes, I wished he would rebel or that he'd stray from the straight and narrow. Just a little."

"Is that what you think I am? Jack's rebellion? Jack's walk on the wild side?" *Jack's illicit thrill, to be put aside when he comes to his senses?* No, he would never believe that, but it didn't stop his stomach from turning to ice.

"No, I don't. He did the right thing in helping you because that's the type of man he is. A good man. But what's happened has gone beyond the boundaries of help, wouldn't you say? I applaud that he gave you the assistance you needed, but I don't want him feeling obligated."

Rory's heart shrivelled.

"Obligated?" Rory rasped. "I'd rather walk away and not look back if I believed that obligation was all that binds us together."

Was everything he and Jack were building together nothing more than Jack feeling sorry for him? No. He wouldn't and couldn't think that. He loved Jack as much as he knew Jack loved him, and he was going to make damn sure Diana knew it as well.

"I know I'm not what you'd have hoped for Jack, and I'm not just talking about the circumstances that brought us together. I'm not very well educated, and I've not got a high-flying professional job. I was brought up in a care home until I was adopted by a couple who in the end couldn't wait to get rid of me. All I've got to my name is a qualification from a second-rate catering college and a badly paid job in a local bakery. I don't have anything, but at the same time I have everything. I have Jack's love, and he has mine, and for us that's all that matters."

Everything he'd said, he'd said from the heart and meant each and every word. Whether or not Diana believed him, he didn't know, and there was nothing he could do if she didn't. He would never, ever hurt Jack; he and Jack knew that one simple truth and in the end it was all that mattered.

They sat in silence, looking at each other over the abandoned breakfast. Half-drunk tea and half-eaten plates of food lay like the debris of a battle in which neither side was the victor.

"Rory, who your family is or isn't, or where you work isn't my concern, whatever you may think. And I'm sorry you found yourself in the position you did, for whatever reason. Nobody should be without a decent roof over their head. But my concern is and always will be my son. If it wasn't, what sort of mother would I be?"

Rory pushed his chair back and stood on legs he feared would buckle beneath him.

"And what sort of man would I be if I only saw Jack as the meal ticket you seem to think I do? You don't know me at all, Diana. But you don't know Jack either. Once, maybe, but not anymore."

## CHAPTER SEVEN

"Are you going to tell me what happened?" Jack glanced over at Rory, trudging up the hill next to him as they headed towards the Tor.

"What do you mean?"

"Come on, Ro. . ."

Jack had been on the verge of getting up when Rory had walked into the bedroom. Rory's face had been bleached of all colour, and he'd mumbled something about having gone downstairs for some breakfast before he'd dived into the en-suite bathroom. He hadn't looked much better when he emerged several minutes later. Something had disagreed with him, and Jack very much doubted it would have been the estate-produced sausages or bacon. When he suggested they go out, Rory had nodded as relief glimmered in his eyes.

They escaped the house without seeing anybody

and headed for the Tor. Rory had said next to nothing as they made their way up the steep hill. It was a tough climb, and soon both were out of breath, giving Jack the perfect excuse to chew over how he was going to get Rory to open up.

Sod it. If he had to be blunt, then so be it.

"Has my mum been questioning you? My dad'll be home later, and I think it'd be best all round if we tell them outright. It'd clear the—"

Rory stopped, pulling Jack to a standstill next to him.

"I told her. I told her how we met. I told her about living on the streets and being destitute."

"Oh," Jack said, taken aback by Rory's blurted-out words. "But how? And why? You didn't have to do this on your own, and I didn't want you to." *What the fuck has happened for it to come all pouring out?*

"I know, but—the time was right. I couldn't *not* tell her, Jack."

Rory looked down, and Jack swore he could hear the cogs turning in Rory's head.

Jack placed a finger under Rory's chin and eased his head up. "I want you to tell me exactly what happened." It took all Jack's self-restraint to keep his voice steady. A conversation that was never going to be easy, even with the two of them, had been had by Rory alone. *No bloody wonder he'd looked like he was about to throw up when he'd walked into the bedroom.*

"She's worried I might be. . . taking advantage of you."

"What?" Ice filled Jack's veins. "What the hell does she think she's playing at?"

"Jack, please. Please, just listen to me?"

Rory was shaking his arm, but the only thing Jack was aware of was a cold, hard anger binding its ropes around him.

"Jack?"

Jack stared at Rory, the pleading he saw in his boyfriend's eyes the one thing stopping him from racing back to the house to demand to know what the hell Diana was doing before bundling Rory into the car and hightailing it without a backwards glance.

"Tell me what happened. Leave nothing out."

Everything inside Jack, his heart, his stomach, his lungs, shrivelled and turned in on themselves as Rory told him what had taken place in the warm and homely kitchen.

"I have to confront her on this. I can't leave it." Jack's voice was low and gravelly as he ground out each and every word. "And then we'll go back to London."

"No."

"Are you saying I shouldn't confront her? I'm sorry, Ro, but there's no way she's getting away with this."

"No, I mean I don't want – or I don't think – we should go back home. It'd be like we were running away, and she'd think her suspicions are right and that I'd forced you to leave. I don't want that, Jack. I don't want that for me, but more I don't want it for you. She's your mum, and as much as she's so wrong about me and about us, I don't want to be the wedge that comes between you both."

Jack stared down into Rory's pleading, beseeching eyes.

"How can you even want to stay here, after that?" Jack whispered. "She insulted you, Ro, and she accused me of being some kind of imbecile who's incapable of making his own decisions. I won't stand by and accept that. I'm sorry, but if I'm going to have some kind of relationship with my mother after today, I have to sort this out one way or the other." What had happened to the open- and fair-minded woman he'd always told Rory his mother was? As he stood with Rory, on the brow of the windswept hill, Jack questioned whether she had, in fact, really existed.

"Just think before you say anything. For me? Please, Jack? I want us not to just claw back from this but to rise above it. We won't do that by running back to London – not that I didn't want to do just that – but I'd blame myself if you said something to her you later regretted."

"Regretted?" The word burst from Jack's tongue. The only thing he regretted at the moment was ever subjecting Rory to his mother. Jack sucked in a deep breath. "Okay. I'll talk to her when I'm calm and I'll behave like the rational adult she clearly thinks I'm not. Come on, let's get up this bloody hill."

# CHAPTER EIGHT

As they made for the tall, granite tower, which had stood for over two hundred years, Jack tried to pull his rampaging thoughts back into some kind of order.

He was *not* going to let what had happened go unchallenged. Who Rory was and the life they were building together were too important for him not to retaliate when attacked.

But how to do it? He had one shot at making his position clear: Rory was out of bounds. Any intimation, any suggestion, any slur on Rory's character was a slur on *his*. It was a message that had to be delivered cold and clear. As much as he loved his mother, although that love was currently stretched thin, he'd walk away if he had to make a choice. It'd rip him to shreds inside, but he'd do it and not look back. Diana needed to understand the stakes, and there was only one person walking the Earth who had the power to make that happen, and he would be coming home that evening.

His father.

The Tor had been designed to hark back to the Middle Ages. Spongy green and yellow moss stuck to the walls, and ivy wound its way up upwards. Recessed into the wall facing them was a heavy wooden door, its top coming to a point like the door of an old church. They hadn't spoken again about what had happened, as though agreeing without saying to put the matter aside for a while. Jack's decision to speak to and seek the guidance of the man who'd been his rock from the day he'd been born had calmed both Jack's anger and his heart rate.

Jack pulled the long iron key from his jacket pocket and slipped it into the lock. As he pushed his shoulder to it, the door opened with a long, low creak. They stepped inside, and Jack turned on a dim light and stood aside.

"Oh, wow."

Rory looked around him, his mouth agape and his eyes wide. Jack smiled, not just because Rory's reaction was the same as everybody else's who saw the inside of the Tor for the first time, but because the beauty and outright strangeness of the place, had for a moment, it seemed, pushed all Rory's worries aside.

"What are these?" Rory looked from the walls to Jack and back to the walls.

"They're the Knights of the Round Table. The whole place is a tribute to the Arthurian legend." Jack stepped up behind Rory and coiled his arms around his waist.

"They're huge. And also kind of weird and creepy. I feel like they're watching me."

Rory shivered. Jack hugged him closer and kissed the top of his head. He knew exactly what Rory meant. Every knight was at least three times life-size but had been painted with such skill each figure seemed poised, as though at any second they would come alive and spring into action.

"They scared me to death as a kid, especially that one." Jack pointed to a black-haired knight with sharp features and cunning foxy eyes. There was a cruelty to the features that still had the power to send a shiver down his spine. "There was a big round table here as well, but that was years ago and before I was born. George, the bastard," Jack said, referring to his elder brother, "locked me in here one time because I'd caught him smoking dope and threatened to tell my parents. He only told them where I was when they were about to form a search party to look for me. They grounded him for a month."

"Did you tell them about the dope?" Rory asked, turning around and looking up at Jack.

"You think I was a snitch? I'm distraught. Come on, let's climb to the top because the view's amazing."

Jack pulled Rory to a low opening in one of the walls, and together they climbed the narrow stone spiral staircase. At the top, Jack produced another key and, with the help of a hard shove, pushed open the door.

Rory gazed about him. "You're so lucky to have been brought up somewhere like this. I can't imagine what it must have been like."

The view from the top of the Tor was breathtaking. Rolling fields dotted with sheep spread out all around them. In one direction, lush pasture turned to the stark, barren uplands of Dartmoor; in the other and on the distant horizon, lay the sea.

Jack leaned against the wall and watched as Rory made his way around the top of the tower, leaning over the parapet and drinking in the lush scenery. Colour glazed Rory's pale skin, and a smile as warm as his eyes lit up his face, melting the last vestiges of tension.

"I can't even see a road," Rory said, coming up to Jack and slinging his arms around him. "It's like we're the only two people left in the world."

"George used to bring his girlfriends up here, and Caroline told me she popped her cherry on these very flagstones. She was pissed when she came out with that little gem and now denies all knowledge of the conversation, but it's one I like to keep as ammo. It's whispered that I was conceived out here, under a full moon. That's one conversation I *won't* be having with my parents."

"So the Tor is just one massive aphrodisiac?"

Jack smiled as Rory's eyes widened.

"And what about you?"

"What about me?"

"Any tales to tell?"

"I was always too scared of the place. But I'm a big boy now, so maybe it's time I rectified that."

Rory tightened his arms around Jack and pulled himself in closer.

"I've always enjoyed outdoor pursuits," Rory murmured as he pressed a kiss to Jack's lips.

Jack groaned as Rory ground his growing arousal against his own. He closed his eyes as Rory nibbled, sucked, and licked at the tender, nervy skin at the base of his earlobe, and he shivered and squirmed, each delicious scrape of Rory's teeth or sweep of his tongue sending shock waves over his skin.

"Ro—"

A sudden shove, and Jack was pinned with this

back to the chest-high parapet.

The shocked and worried Rory of earlier was nowhere to be seen. *Maybe this is what he needs, to feel in control, to be the attacker and not the attacked. Anything you need, Ro, anything. . .*

Jack gasped. His jeans and briefs were shoved down over his hips, freeing his desperate, eager cock.

"Oh fuck, Ro." Jack groaned when Rory wrapped his hand around his shaft, and swept his thumb over the slit, sliding through the pooling pre-cum.

"Hmmm, very nice." Laughter trickled through Rory's words.

Jack's heart hammered, captivated by Rory's pink, wet tongue lapping the juice from his thumb pad.

"*Ro. . .*" Jack's voice was little more than a thin whine, and he shuddered in delicious anticipation of what Rory would be lapping at next as he thrust his fingers into Rory's thick, heavy hair and pushed down.

"Don't think so."

Jack was spun round so fast he almost lost his balance.

"These flagstones would be murder on the knees."

Jack shivered, and his breath hitched as Rory's whispered words and his warm, damp breath, wafted over his ear.

"But we've not—"

"Never fear, Rory's here." Rory chuckled. He

stepped back, taking with him the warmth of his body, a warmth Jack ached to have pressed into him.

A rummage through a pocket, the rip of a packet, and Jack's intake of breath as the cool lube was smeared around his hot and nervy entrance. They'd dispensed with the need for condoms just a few weeks before, and thank fuck for that, Jack thought as he closed his eyes and shuddered out a breath as Rory's long, thin fingers massaged, easing and relaxing the muscle with every stroke.

Jack's knees almost bucked beneath him when Rory swept his tongue over his ear, captured the lobe, and sucked hard.

"Fuck, Ro. For somebody who's so—aahhh!"

*Sweet.* The word was swept away by Jack's gasp as Rory bit down, sending a tsunami of shock waves raging through every nerve in his body. With the face of an angel and big, dark eyes that were often less doe than devil when they closed the bedroom door, it was a side to Rory's nature that had revealed itself one night in an explosion of want and need, leaving Jack reeling, breathless, and wanting more.

"You ready?" Rory murmured into Jack's ear.

Jack could only nod. He clenched his arse cheeks, holding tight for several seconds as Rory kissed and nipped at his neck before he released, and his relaxed muscle allowed Rory to push forward.

Jack gasped as his body quivered and tensed as he teetered on the tightrope of stretch and burn.

"I've got you, Jack. I won't let you fall." Rory's whispered words were all he needed. Rory had him safe. It was all he needed to know.

Rory's hands clamped to his hips, his fingers pressing hard into Jack's flesh. *I'll have bruises later. . .* but the thought faded as everything was driven from his mind as Rory drove into his body.

Nothing slow, nothing gentle, this was about a fast and furious fuck. And Jack wanted it. He wanted to be pummelled and driven to the edge. He wanted to forget about everything and everybody. He wanted to forget it all, except for the man who was pushing deeper and deeper into his body just as he pushed deeper and deeper into his heart.

"Oh, fuck!" Jack's yell split the silent air. If he knew, he didn't care as his nerves screamed out as Rory hit his gland, over and over and over. He wasn't going to last. All it would take would be one final push for him to tumble and fall into oblivion. Jack wrapped his hand around his dick, pumping in time to Rory's furious tempo. His balls tingled and tightened as heat seared through him, sending him shuddering to the edge.

"Ro. . ." It was as much as Jack could groan out as Rory's rapid, out-of-control breathing and his ground-out, incomprehensible words burst into a cry that echoed around them as he slammed forward and flooded into Jack. The explosion of wet heat was the shove that sent Jack tumbling, falling, falling, and falling, and crashing to the ground.

"Christ." Jack clung to the rim of the parapet, willing his wobbly legs not to give up on him, but Rory's arms, tight around his waist, held him fast. The kiss that butterflied on the back of his neck was followed by a soft nuzzle that sent ripples of warmth through his chest.

"Do you think it's the country air?" Rory panted into Jack's neck. "Hold on. I've just got to. . ." Rory pulled away.

Moments later, they were tugging up jeans, fastening zips, and buckling up belts. Jack stuffed the balled-up wet and sticky tissues deep into the pocket of his jacket.

"So you've got a Tor story too."

Jack gazed down into Rory's flushed and smiling face and cupped his palms to Rory's cheeks.

"Yes, I have. It's the best one because of who helped me write it."

Jack pressed his lips to Rory's in a long, slow, languorous kiss as the birds swept, swooped, and circled above them in the warm spring sunshine.

## CHAPTER NINE

The little tea shop could have come straight from the set of a TV cosy mystery, where every home was a thatched cottage, and everybody smiled and said good morning in between murdering each other or committing other heinous crimes behind crisp lace curtains.

Jack hadn't wanted to spoil the afterglow from the Tor by chancing running into his mother at the house. Beneath his surface calm, he was still seething. He wouldn't be able to bite his tongue, and he wasn't sure that was the smart way forward. Until his dad was home, the best policy was to steer clear, and that meant jumping into the car and heading out into the lush countryside.

"What did you think?" Jack asked, nodding

towards the empty cake stand in the middle of the little round table.

"Wonderful. Scones and traditional cakes, if they're done well, are unbeatable in my opinion. And they sell well too. Victoria sponge, lemon drizzle, and carrot cake consistently outsell fancy cupcakes with weird flavour combos or fussy patisserie."

Rory shifted in his seat and sat up taller as he warmed to his theme. Jack suppressed a smile. Engaged and enthusiastic about what he knew and loved, this was exactly how he wanted and needed Rory to be.

"It's not really the kind of thing Arturo's does, is it?" Jack asked, keeping his voice as neutral as he could.

Rory huffed and shook his head. "No. And that makes him short-sighted about his business, in my view. I've tried to persuade Arturo to extend his range, but all he does is give me a condescending smile. Because he knows best. Apparently. But the carrot cake I made was gone by lunchtime. Every crumb of it. It outsold all his usual range hands down, and that's got to say something." Rory slumped back. "His place does well, but even in the short time I've been there, I've seen a change in what people want. There are fads and fashions in food as much as in anything, but he won't listen, and he's made it clear he doesn't welcome *my intervention*, as he puts it."

"Maybe he sees you as competition. You showed you could do better, and he doesn't like it."

"I don't know," Rory said with a shrug. "I just find it frustrating that he's not keeping his finger on the pulse of changing tastes or the paying public's yearning for nostalgia, which means all those firm favourites when it comes to cakes and pastries. The shop's in a prime location, the right demographic is there on his doorstep and with money to spend, but he's not responding to any of it. But what do I know? I'm there to serve coffee and plate up."

"It doesn't have to be that way." Jack concentrated on pouring them both more tea from the chintzy teapot.

"Of course it does, for as long as I work there. It's his business, so I have to dance to his tune. Despite my frustrations, I like working for an independent."

"You could be your own independent."

"What?"

Jack put the teapot down and met Rory's eyes, seeing confusion in their chocolate-brown depths.

"You could be your own independent," he repeated. "You could run your own business."

"Run my. . . but. . ."

"Look," Jack said, taking Rory's hands in his. "As you said, it's Arturo tune. The thing is, it's not one you're happy dancing to."

"It's not that bad."

"Isn't it? You were thrilled when he let you do some baking, but that only happened because he was in a fix and you were able to help him out."

Jack smiled as he recalled how excited Rory was to be cooking professionally again, but his smile fell away when he also remembered how fed up Rory had been when Arturo had rebuffed his attempts to persuade him to allow him to make the step up from general assistant to baker.

"You could be an asset to his business, but he won't let it happen. But you could be your *own* asset, Rory. If that's what you want, I can help make it happen." Jack held Rory's gaze, just as he held his hands, and waited for understanding to dawn.

"You know it's what I want, but—"

"Why should there be a *but?* You could have your own place, run on your terms. I don't want to see your talent unused and your enthusiasm eroded and chipped away. That's what'll happen if you stay at Arturo's, and it'll happen again if you move on to another bakery. It *won't* happen if you have your own business, run your way."

"I don't know what to—"

"Say? Do? You might not, but I do. But it needs to be your decision. Whatever you decide, I'll be with you every step of the way. I want you to put aside what you feel you should or shouldn't do and think about this for the serious business proposition it is."

"I've never run a business. I wouldn't know where to start."

From the moment Jack had planted the seed, Rory hadn't been able to think of anything else. He hadn't said much as they'd toured the pretty countryside, fed the birds gathered around the pond in yet another picture-postcard village, or gazed out towards the rugged moorland from ancient stone footbridges spanning fast-flowing streams and brooks. His thoughts were as tumultuous and tumbled as the rushing waters but nowhere near as clear. Jack said nothing more, sensing, Rory knew, that he was having to make sense of it in his own head.

As they'd made their way back to The Manor House, he'd stared out of the car window, lurching from the excitement of the wealth of possibilities he could see opening up before him to outright terror. The two extremes had come to an out-and-out fist fight, leaving Terror the victor – at least until Possibilities had roused, staggered up to standing, and declared itself not yet dead.

"No, but you know your product and the market.

You know what people want but also what they're likely to want in the future. If you can anticipate trends—"

"Nostalgia for traditional cakes and pastries, fuelled by the nation's obsession with bake-off shows?" Rory smiled as he said it. They were talking about – well, cakes and pastries. Market predictions were for... Rory didn't know what they were for. It was the kind of thing that was said by grey-suited economists on the TV, which always made him switch off. *But wasn't it me who was talking about emerging trends and demographics earlier?*

"And why not? Finger on the pulse, remember? That's business gold. For the rest of it, you talk to those who are already making a success of it, and you emulate them. Where you lack experience in the mechanics of running a business, you just buy it in."

"You make it sound so easy, but you've forgotten one thing."

"What's that?"

"I don't have anything like the money needed to get myself off the ground. With just a part-time job in the service industry, no bank is going to give me a second look."

"The Bank of Jack de Lacy is ready and willing to place a bet."

"Jack, it's a wonderful and generous offer." Rory

placed his hand on Jack's cheek, feeling the scratch of stubble against his palm as Jack nuzzled into him.

They lay on their sides on Jack's bed, their legs entwined and knotted around each other's. When they'd arrived back at the house, they'd been greeted by Badger's excited bark and furiously wagging tail, but otherwise there had been silence. They'd headed up the sweeping staircase, eschewing the Morning Room, the kitchen, and a host of other rooms in the rambling manor. Badger had followed, ignoring Jack's command to stay downstairs and choosing instead to stick close to Rory and follow his every step. Once inside, the young dog had plonked itself in front of the door, all snuffles and yelps and twitching tail as he sunk into a doggy dream.

"No, it's not," Jack said, clamping his hand over Rory's. "Well, okay, it is, but that's not what's important. Rory, it makes sound business sense. Where we live, the people who spend good money – and a lot of it – are moving in in droves. The yummy mummy types I suppose you could call them. Affluent young families. The sort who'll pay premium prices for the right product – the product you know. I think if we get the right advice, talk to the right people, we could have something amazing on our hands."

Terror called it a day and said it was time for a nap,

as Possibilities jumped up and down and punched the air.

Jack's enthusiasm was contagious, but it wasn't that which caught at Rory's heart and held it tight. It was Jack's belief in him, his belief that he could really do this, could be the success he'd always yearned to be. Nobody had ever had the confidence in him that Jack did, and that included Rory himself. *You can't do this. You can't do that.* He'd been told those words in one form after another for so many years by everybody who'd drifted through his life that Rory had taken them as truth, their dead weight pinning him to the ground. Yet here was Jack, smiling into his eyes and promising him he could fly.

"We? Do you have that much faith in me? Really?" Rory whispered.

Jack nodded, his eyes never leaving Rory's for a moment.

"Yes, *we*. Because we'd be in it together. Me and you, every inch of the way. You're a sure bet, Rory Kincaid. Do you honestly think I'd take a risk if you weren't?"

Rory closed his eyes as Jack leaned in and kissed him. Slow, soft, and sweet, Jack's kiss tasted of the promise of a life Rory had thought would never, could never, be his.

“Jack,” Rory breathed against Jack's warm lips. “I—”

Badger's frantic, excited bark and his scrabbling and snuffling at the door, shattering the honeyed silence, had Rory and Jack almost leaping off the bed.

“Fucking hell.” Jack slapped his palms to his chest. “That dog almost gave me a heart attack.”

“I think Badger's got a friend,” Rory said as the deeper, growly bark of another dog sounded from the wide hallway on the other side of the door.

“That's Bruno. Dad's dog,” Jack added. “If he's roaming around and barking, it means Dad's home.”

# CHAPTER TEN

"Good to see you, Jack. It's been far too long. I know you have your busy life in London, but try and get down a bit more often, eh? Your mother misses you terribly."

Sir Roger. Patriarch and head of the ancient De Lacy family. Custodian of the estate for future generations, savvy businessman, Justice of the Peace, and former county Lord Lieutenant. Roger was those things and more, but most important of all, he was Dad.

"Well, come and sit down and tell me all your news. And where's your young chap, by the way?" Roger settled himself into a wing-backed chair, old and shabby with age, looking around him as if expecting to see Rory hiding in a shadowy corner of the library.

Jack settled himself opposite. The library was his

father's domain, a place of peace and refuge he'd always claimed.

"He's in the conservatory."

"Why's he in there? You should have brought him through with you."

"You will meet him and soon. But I needed to speak to you first. Alone."

"Alone, eh? Why do I think this calls for a stiff drink? Pour a couple of scotches."

Jack did as he was bid. Sitting back down, he stared into his glass, swirling it around and releasing the earthy, rich peat aroma underscored with burnt caramel. He could feel his father's eyes on him. It was now or never. Jack put the glass down without tasting a drop and looked up to meet his father's gaze.

"There's been an incident. Between Mum and Rory."

"Go on." Roger's voice was calm and as rich and deep as the whisky he nursed.

As briefly and succinctly as he could, Jack told his father what had taken place earlier that day.

"She all but accused Rory of being some kind of gold digger, of latching on to me for his own gain. I was furious because he's not and he isn't. I wanted to confront her and then go back to London, but Rory persuaded me not to. But I'm still angry, Dad. This isn't something that can be overlooked because it'll fester. I don't want that, but I won't accept her slandering Rory, because that's what it is." Jack leaned forward, resting his arms on his knees, never flinching from his father's steady and serious gaze. "He has to be welcomed into the family wholeheartedly and accepted for who he is. If he's not, it means I won't be coming back here."

Jack's heart twisted. The home he was born in, where he grew up, the village; they'd been the backdrop to a happy upbringing. And his family, who he'd loved and had loved him in return and without condition. Was he willing to turn his back on it all? If Rory was made to feel he couldn't be a part of it, then yes. Jack would pay the price, and he'd do it without a second thought.

Silence filled the air around them. Jack watched as his father sipped and savoured his whisky. Roger's eyes narrowed, and his brow puckered. It was Roger's *thinking face*, and Jack knew to wait for his father to give voice to his thoughts.

"Are you quite sure Rory's interpretation was the correct one?"

"Yes. He told me she said I had a tendency to make bad decisions about what she called affairs of the heart and that Rory had come into my life when I was vulnerable." Jack shook his head, pushing down the anger that once more was heating up in the pit of his belly. "I'm not the wet-behind-the-ears kid ripe for being made a fool of she thinks I am."

Jack shifted in his seat. It was *exactly* what he'd been with Sam, his cheating, conniving ex, but that was a different man and a different life.

"Your mother's already spoken to me."

"What?" Jack reared back.

"She was most upset."

"*She* was upset? She doesn't know the fucking meaning of the word." Jack jumped up as the embers of his anger burst into flame. His mother had waded in with her nasty insinuations and was now claiming that it was *she* who was upset?

"Jack, sit down."

Roger's voice, as calm as ever but underlined with iron. Rarely heard, it was a voice to be obeyed, but Jack wasn't a kid anymore.

"Why should I, Dad? And why should we stay here a moment longer?"

"Because we want you to. Please, Jack, sit down," Roger said, his voice softer.

Jack slumped back down into his seat.

"Your mother knows she made a grave error."

Jack huffed. "I think fuck-up is the term you're looking for."

"Are you going to allow me to continue?"

Roger's voice was cool and unruffled, unaffected by Jack's outburst.

"Yes. I apologise," Jack mumbled, accepting the mild reprimand.

Roger took another sip of whisky, taking his time. Jack waited, his skin prickling in anticipation. Roger placed his glass down on the small table next to his chair and settled back.

"Your mother realises she mishandled the conversation, but she maintains it was a conversation that needed to happen—"

"We were going to tell you—"

Roger raised a hand, and Jack fell into silence.

"We have no doubt you had every intention of doing that. Your mother jumped the gun, as it were. She saw an opportunity to speak to Rory and made a complete mess of it. But she stands by needing to voice her concerns, although she regrets the manner in which she did it. Jack, hear me out."

Jack had opened his mouth to speak, snapping it shut under his father's steady gaze.

"Both your mother and I knew you and Sam weren't suited. We said nothing because you were a grown man, and it wasn't our place to make our views known. But you never seemed happy, Jack, not deep down, and it was hard, so damn hard, not to step in. I'll be candid. When the two of you finished, we were relieved. Despite your brave face and your insistence that all was well, we both knew that was not the case. We're your parents, Jack, and we know you, just like we know Caroline and George."

"I don't understand what this has got to do with Rory and why she said what she did."

"Don't you? I think if you step back and take a dispassionate look at the events of earlier, you will understand. It doesn't mean you'll be any happier, but you'll *understand*, and that's what you'll need to do to make this first visit of Rory's the success we all – and I mean all – want it to be. Jack, whatever you may think, your mother was correct when she said Rory came into your life when you were at a low point. You hadn't long come out of a serious relationship, even one we thought wasn't right for you, so of course you weren't going to be at your best. We were both disappointed you didn't confide in us and chose instead to maintain that your life had taken a sudden and miraculous turn for the better. Which we very much doubted, I should add."

"What? You knew?"

Jack's face prickled with heat. He'd been dumped and cheated on not just by his boyfriend but by his best friend. He'd felt stupid and gullible and had hugged his hurt to his chest. Instead of turning to those who'd loved him without question, he'd sought to prop up his injured pride by laying claim to a non-existent relationship with a new boyfriend, in the weeks before Rory had stumbled into his life.

"Let's just say we had our suspicions. When Rory told your mother how the pair of you met and when, it didn't take a lot of detective work to realise Rory wasn't the chap you'd claimed to have met. You'd been batting away any questions about this supposed new friend of yours for some weeks before Christmas. We had our suspicions this chap you'd told us you'd met was, well let's just say expedient, and Rory confirmed it without realising."

Jack's lips twisted into a rueful smile. His lies, to bolster his flagging self-esteem and confidence, had fooled nobody – even his parents, miles away, deep in the Devonshire countryside.

"I still can't accept what she said to Rory and the way she did it. She owes him and me an apology, Dad."

"She certainly does for how she handled the situation. But for her concerns? I'm not so sure. Your mother, like anybody else and that includes you, is entitled to their views."

"Even though she's wrong? Even though she thinks Rory's just out to get what he can out of me?" The flames in the pit of Jack's stomach grew hotter.

"That was clumsy and insensitive of her and groundless. What your mother thinks of as being forthright is often—well, rather more than that. She was worried because she doesn't want to see you get hurt again. It's because she loves you, never forget that, and misguided though her actions were, they were the actions of any good mother — any good parent. If you have children yourself, one day, you'll understand. And you would do exactly what she did. Well, perhaps not *exactly*. . ." Roger shrugged before picking up and finishing his scotch.

"But will she apologise?"

"Yes, I believe she will, but she'll do it in her own way. If you attempt to force her into a corner, she'll dig her heels in all the more. "

Jack barked out a short, hard laugh as he shook his head.

"If you believe I'm going to join in some sort of crucifixion of your mother, Jack, for voicing her concerns – however poorly carried out – I'm afraid you're very much mistaken. It's been a difficult start for both of them, but don't let it taint the rest of your stay here – and more importantly, Rory's. Now, I think it's about time I met this young man of yours, don't you?"

## CHAPTER ELEVEN

Curled up on the sofa in the corner of the potted plant-filled conservatory, Rory stared through the glass walls to the manicured lawn and the flower beds beyond. Late afternoon sunshine streamed in, filling the room with rich, buttery light. Save for the tick of an ornamental clock, it was silent, unlike the riot of thoughts running through Rory's head.

*What a day.*

First, the conversation with Diana. Rory shuddered. He didn't have to relish it, but he'd face up to his next encounter with his head held high. On its own, it would have been more than enough for one day, but when Jack had made his proposition, Rory had been floored.

A bakery of his own. Maybe not just a bakery but a café too in time. A business he could pour all his passion into, and Jack would be with him all the way. It was thrilling and exciting, and he should be grabbing the offer with both hands and holding on tight. *But. . .* Jack had said there should be no buts, but how could there not be?

Doubt had crept in and had begun to whisper. *Setting up a business is a huge expense. . . most new ventures fail within a year. . . and what do you know about business. . . what if you lost Jack all his money. . . what if you lost Jack. . . his parents wouldn't like the idea, would they. . . they'd just think you wanted Jack for what you could get out of him. . .* Round and round it went. As soon as Rory pushed one thought aside, another would sneak in and take its place.

The door creaked open, and Rory turned around, hoping to find Jack. Instead, Anne came in holding a tray.

"Young Master Jack asked me to bring you tea. I've also taken the liberty of providing a selection of biscuits, Mr Rory. All home-made," Anne added, a note of pride in her broad Devonian accent.

*Master Jack? Did she really just call him* Master *Jack?* "Did he? Oh, thank you."

Anne smiled as she bustled around, setting out the tea things on a standing tray.

"Will there be anything more, Mr Rory?" Anne

asked, giving him an inquisitive look as she finished pouring the tea.

"Erm, no. And please, it's just Rory. All this," he said, looking around the conservatory, "it's not the world I come from, but then you probably guessed that already."

Anne's eyes crinkled as she smiled down at him.

"If that's what you'd rather. It's just that the other—I'm sorry, I shouldn't—please forgive my indiscretion." Anne's already ruddy cheeks turned an even deeper shade of red.

"The other? Do you mean Jack's last boyfriend? Sam?"

Anne nodded, her eyes flitting around.

"Yes. He was always very particular about being addressed as Mr Sam, so--"

"You thought I would be too? Then all the more reason *not* to call me that." Rory gave Anne what he hoped was a reassuring smile.

"Thank you. Rory. Master Jack said he'd come and find you. He's with Sir Roger at the moment. Is there anything else I can get for you?"

"No, I'm fine."

With another smile, a moment later she was gone.

Rory picked up one of the biscuits and bit into its crumbly, butter-filled richness and chewed slowly, savouring as he thought.

Sam. Pompous and arrogant. Yes, he'd insist on being called Mr Sam. Rory had had the misfortune to meet him a couple of times soon after he'd walked into Jack's life. It was a couple of times too many.

*It feels like a lifetime ago.* And it was, he supposed. His life had changed out of all recognition and was about to change again if Jack had anything to do with it.

The snuffling whimper at his side pulled Rory from his thoughts. He couldn't help smiling when he looked at the young dog, who'd sneaked up onto the sofa and had curled up beside him. Another little whimper, a sweep of his pink tongue, and a turn of his head from Rory to the biscuit and back again told Rory all he needed to know.

"That is the most blatant display of cupboard love I have ever come across. Here, have this." Rory dropped the rest of the biscuit into the dog's mouth. It was gone in a second. "I'm sure Anne would have a fit if she knew I was feeding you her excellent biscuits, but I won't tell if you don't."

"I'm sure she'd be delighted. It's not just the human members of the family Anne likes to feed."

Rory leapt up from the sofa, sending Badger tumbling with a loud and high-pitched yelp as he crashed into the standing tray. The whole thing smashed to the floor, leaving the fine china in pieces and tea soaking into the threadbare and no doubt very old and very expensive rug. Broken biscuits lay everywhere, each one of them eagerly lapped up by a now recovered Badger.

"Er—" It was the only sound Rory could make.

A low, rumbling laugh filled the room, so like Jack's it was uncanny.

"Tea, coffee, and a whole lot more beside has been spilt over this rug by both the two- and four-legged amongst us. Rory, I'm pleased to meet you at last. I'm Roger, Jack's father, as I'm sure you've already guessed," he said, offering his hand.

Rory clenched his teeth so as not to wince when Roger clasped his hand in a brief but strong grip.

"Hello. I'm sorry about. . ." Rory looked down at the chaos spread around him, burning with embarrassment. Whatever Roger said, it wasn't the best way to make a first impression, but the older man just waved his hand as if it wasn't even worth mentioning as he went over to a cabinet and picked up the phone that sat on top and made a short call.

"Dean will come and clear it up," Roger said, his tone clipped but not unfriendly. Still, Rory had to resist the impulse to say *Yes, Sir. Of course, Sir.*

A few moments later, a chunky young man who Rory hadn't seen before turned up, but he looked so much like Anne he was surely her son. Roger nodded towards a collection of mismatched chairs close to the door leading to the veranda, where they each took a seat.

"I've just been speaking to Jack, as I know you're aware. He told me Diana rather cornered you." Roger's focus was steady, his eyes as blue as Jack's.

"Yes. Erm, we had, I mean. . ." Rory's voice trailed off.

*For God's sake.* He'd already made a fool of himself over the smashed tea service. If he had any hope of making some kind of reasonable impression on at least one of Jack's parents, he had to rise to the challenge he saw in the intelligent, assessing eyes of the man who sat opposite him. Rory straightened his back and forced himself not to flinch.

"Yes, she did. She hijacked me and made insinuations she can't back up. And are downright wrong. I don't think that was on."

Roger's brows shot up towards his thinning hairline.

*You see that, Rog? The De Lacys aren't the only ones who can say what they think.* Rory held his breath as he waited for Roger's response, using all his effort to keep a bland and neutral expression plastered over his face. All those poker games he'd played with his catering college friends hadn't been wasted after all. *One of the most important things to learn is not to let your opponents guess your hand. It's not called poker face for nothing. . .* It was a game Rory had been a complete failure at, but this time he was going to make sure he came out the winner.

"So I understand. And it shouldn't have happened. I trust everybody can move forward."

Was it an apology? Rory was unsure, but whether it was or not, it looked like it was all he was going to get.

"Ah, here's Jack. . ." Roger said, looking over Rory's shoulder towards the door.

Jack came in and made straight for Rory, squeezing his shoulder and looking down into his eyes. *Everything okay?* his look seemed to ask. Rory answered with a barely there nod.

"Have you shown Rory the estate yet?" Roger asked, looking at Jack.

"Some of it. The herb and box gardens—"

"Excellent. And did you introduce Rory to our knights?"

"He did," Rory said. "I've never seen anything like it before."

"There's only one other example in England, I believe." Roger looked at his watch before he pushed himself up to standing, Rory and Jack following. "Diana and I have a dinner engagement in Tavistock." Roger grimaced. "Business, not pleasure, sadly, and likely to be very dull and very long. We're going to have to leave you to your own devices." Roger smiled, warm and friendly, making the resemblance between father and son unmistakable. "Rory, you're very welcome here. I'll see you both tomorrow."

A moment later Roger was gone, and Rory collapsed back down into his seat.

"That was—I don't know what that was if I'm honest."

"Feel a bit shell-shocked?" Jack asked, perching on the armrest and running his fingers through Rory's hair.

"That's one way of putting it. It's been one hell of a rollercoaster of a day. What did he say?"

"Mum had already told him. Apparently she was upset at how she handled it. Dad doesn't want what's happened to ruin the rest of your stay – and she did what she did out of love and concern for me apparently."

"Isn't that what I said, or kind of?"

Jack snorted. "I don't think anything's been resolved, because you're owed a full and proper apology. Not just for what she said but how she said it. The option to pack up and go back to London's still there if you want it. I wouldn't blame you, Ro. Don't suffer in silence on my account."

"No, I've already said. Can we leave it for now? Please?"

Jack shrugged, and the two of them fell into silence for a few moments.

"That bloody dog who's fallen in love with you hasn't pissed all over the rug, has he?" Jack pointed to the large, dark stain.

"I managed to upend all the tea and biscuits, with Badger's help. It wasn't the best way to meet your dad. Is this rug valuable?"

"Probably."

Rory groaned and covered his face with his hands. What a day, and it wasn't even six o'clock.

Jack pulled Rory up to standing.

"Come on, I think we've both had enough. I reckon we deserve pizzas, chocolate cake, and wine. In bed."

## CHAPTER TWELVE

"Jack?"

Jack looked up from his plate of bacon and eggs to see his mother standing in the kitchen doorway. She had an expression etched into her features Jack wasn't sure he'd seen on her before: uncertainty. And she was hovering, when she never hovered.

"Mum."

"Your father and I had a long conversation yesterday," she said, coming into the kitchen and taking a seat opposite Jack.

"I know."

He wanted to berate his mother, tell her she was wrong about Rory and wrong about him too; he wanted to demand an apology, for her to take back her words and with it her suspicions; he wanted the heat of his anger to fire up in his belly, but instead it lay cold and hard in the pit of his stomach.

"Then you know why I said what I did. I realise now I shouldn't have done it in the manner I—"

"You shouldn't have done it at all." Jack shoved his plate away, no longer hungry, and glared at his mother across the table. "You accused him of being a money grabber—"

"That isn't—"

"Isn't it?"

"No! I just want you to be sure about what you're doing. That whole business with Sam was ghastly. And you do wear your heart on your sleeve. I stand by what I said about Rory coming into your life when you were low and fed up—"

"Which made me ripe for cynical, calculated exploitation, you mean? Thanks for the vote of confidence, Mum."

"Oh, Jack. I've got every confidence in you."

Diana reached over, rested her hand on Jack's and squeezed lightly. Jack resisted the urge to pull away; it seemed cruel and wrong, in spite of his anger, in spite of the gross injustice that had been done to Rory, and in spite of his disappointment in the woman who'd always loved him without condition.

"Then show me you have, Mum. Please. This isn't some kind of rebound thing, with Rory. He makes me feel more alive than I've ever felt before. I was living in a kind of half-light, but I never knew it until he came into my life. Rory's brought brightness, warmth, and sunshine into my world, and that's got to be a good thing, hasn't it?"

"Of course it is, but I worry, darling. I worry about George and Caroline too. It doesn't matter how old any of you are, and it never will. . . but you're my youngest child, and. . ."

"Yes, I'm your youngest, but I'm not a child. And you've got to stop treating me as though I were."

Jack eased his hand away from under his mother's and sat back in his chair.

All the fiery anger he wanted to feel, he couldn't. She looked drained, he thought. The estate and everything that went with its success was down to the unstinting and tireless work of his parents.

He'd been born late in their lives, and as he studied his mother, for the first time ever, Jack saw her not as indomitable, strong, and with steely determination but as a woman who was tired and aging. Jack scrubbed his fingers through his short, fair hair. He loved her. In spite of everything, he loved her and wanted her approval and acceptance of the man he loved. But if she couldn't see Rory for the good and sincere person he was, if unfounded suspicion still bound her tight. . .? Then he would have a decision to make. It would pull him to pieces inside, but there could only be one choice.

Jack pushed himself up to standing and, without flinching or wavering, looked down into his mother's eyes.

"You need to trust me, Mum, and you need to trust Rory. If you can't, I'll walk away from you. It's neither a threat nor an ultimatum. It's a statement of fact. I love you, Mum, but I won't let you and what you think come between me and him." Turning, he walked out of the kitchen, blinking away his misted vision as he did so.

Jack snaked an arm around Rory's waist, letting the warmth of Rory's body melt into his, as the blustery wind beat against them.

After he'd walked out of the kitchen, he'd escaped to a half-hidden corner of the herb garden. He'd needed to be alone for a while to let the tumult of emotions raging through him calm and settle before he'd gone back to his and Rory's room and told him he had somewhere special to show him.

"It was a fishing village," Jack said. "The sea had been encroaching for years, but its fate was sealed in a massive storm in the mid-nineteenth century."

At first glance, the crumbly, red cliff face looked the same as the others on the coastline. Until you looked closer. Then the outlines of long-abandoned houses came into view, rooms ripped open, a window into homes which had submitted to the constant onslaught of the rough, Atlantic waves.

"According to the old stories, it was there one day and gone the next. Taken by the sea. When I was a kid, my friends and I used to try and frighten each other by telling stories about ghosts and the undead. The souls of those who perished in the storm that destroyed the village were supposed to walk the earth. It's an old local story and good for telling on a stormy night when the winds are howling and the waves are crashing against the shore."

"When you've had a few drinks, you mean?" Rory smiled up at him.

"It helps."

They walked along the near-deserted beach, nothing much more than gulls swirling overhead and a few people in the far distance. It wasn't the coastline's prettiest beach, the sand more mud brown in colour than golden, but it was one of Jack's favourites. With no beachside cafés and the only access a steep scramble down from the cliff top, most passed it by in favour of easier alternatives.

"It's lovely here. Other-worldly." Rory raised his face to the sun.

Jack smiled. *Other-worldly*. It was a good description, and he felt a tingle of satisfaction that Rory appreciated and understood the place as much as he did.

"It is. I used to come here a lot when I was in my teens, cycling before I learned to drive. Looking back, it was a haven, I suppose, somewhere I was able to think clearly. Nothing seemed quite as overwhelming as when I was at home or school or with my friends." He coughed to clear his rough, dry throat and blinked away his smudged vision.

"Jack? Are you okay?" Rory came to a halt, stopping Jack, whose arm he held.

"I don't know. I—I spoke to my mum earlier, and I gave her an ultimatum, although I said it wasn't."

"Please, Jack, don't—"

"Ro, she either accepts you're in my life to stay, or she doesn't. And there are consequences to not accepting. There's no halfway house."

"I don't want you taking a stance you feel you can't back away from."

"But—"

"No. No *buts*."

"I can't believe you're so reasonable after what she said to you."

"Because somebody's got to be. What she said,

yeah, it upset me, but I didn't let her walk all over me, even though you think I did."

"I never. . ." Jack's words trailed away when Rory met his eye in a challenging stare.

"I won't deny I feel like I've been dumped into choppy waters, but let me navigate through them in my own way, okay? Come on." Rory took Jack's hand in his and pulled him along the beach. "You're not the only one who had a secret place, you know."

"So what was yours, then?" Jack asked, taking up the cue to leave the fractious problem of his mother behind for the time being.

"It was the top floor of the library, which doesn't exactly make it secret, I suppose."

"Library?"

"Yes. It was always quiet because it was the reference section. Just me and a few dozing old people. Because it was the library I knew I'd never see anybody from school." Rory laughed. "I used to look out over the rooftops and think about leaving. Leaving the town, the Kincaids, leaving it all behind and dreaming about who and what I could be."

"They don't have to be dreams, Ro. I can help make them a reality, you know that."

"The bakery?"

"Yes. I meant what I said. Every single word." Jack turned to Rory and looked into his eyes. "You have to think about my proposition for what it is – a serious business consideration. And it's one I'm convinced will fly. But that's not just me talking. I've told you I've spoken to people who know the business and who know what they're talking about. I'm offering a chance for those dreams you had, hiding away in a library, to turn into reality. Because what are the options? To carry on working for somebody who stifles your creativity and talent? If it's not Arturo doing it, it'll be somebody else. Why be second fiddle when you can be conducting the orchestra?"

He couldn't stand by and see Rory's talent, vision, and passion crumble to dust and blow away on the breeze like the rust-red cliffs above them.

"The idca. . . it's scary and exciting. But is it the right time? Wouldn't it just stoke the flames?"

"My mum?"

Rory nodded.

"Remember what you said about navigating choppy seas? Let me pilot this particular boat."

The sun passed behind a cloud, plunging them into gloom as the breeze picked up and blew Rory's hair over his eyes. Jack's stomach pulled into a hard knot as he waited for an answer that would define the next stage of the life they were building. The breeze dropped, and the sun broke through the cloud, and bright, clear light bathed them once more. Rory pushed aside his dark fringe, his eyes as bright and glittering as the sun on the sea, and Jack's heart swelled and filled his chest as Rory smiled up at him and nodded.

"Yes."

Jack pulled Rory to him, holding him tight under the warmth of the sun as the gulls circled and screamed overhead.

# CHAPTER THIRTEEN

"Church. Sandwiches, simnel cake, and hot cross buns, served with tea and coffee in the village hall. We should have included sausage rolls, but too late now. Easter egg hunt in the herb garden this afternoon for the under fourteens." Diana ticked the items off on her fingers at the same time Caroline ticked them off on a list on an A4 note pad.

Jack stretched his legs under the kitchen table and wondered whether or not to have another cup of tea.

He'd thought long and hard about what Rory had said, the day before when they'd walked along the beach. . . *dumped into choppy waters, but let me navigate through them in my own way*. . . Was he trying too hard to protect Rory? Was he not giving him enough credit about standing up to his mother and meeting her head-on? But it was difficult not to try and protect him.

Jack sighed and topped up his mug from the old chipped, brown teapot, which sat in the middle of the kitchen table.

"Penny for them, little brother?" Caroline smiled at him, her eyes bright and inquisitive.

Jack shook his head, throwing a glance his mother's way.

When he'd come down to the kitchen, he'd found his mother alone, sitting at the table, her note pad detailing the busy day ahead forgotten and abandoned as she'd stared out of the window, deep in thought. She'd made tea for them both, and they'd sat and made small talk. Neither mentioned the conversation of the previous day, but after pouring their second cup, Diana had leaned towards him, her habitual poise and assurance slipping away for a moment, as she'd inhaled a deep breath. Whatever she had been about to say, Jack wasn't to find out as Caroline bustled into the kitchen, declaring she couldn't possibly face the day ahead without caffeine as she'd grabbed a mug and helped herself to the contents of the teapot.

"Will Rory be joining us at church?" Caroline asked, her head bowed as she carried on making notes.

"Yes, he said he would, but I told him it wasn't obligatory."

Caroline looked up, and Jack met his sister's eye. Only family or those who were on the cusp of joining the De Lacy clan made the Good Friday procession along St Peter's nave.

"Unless he's Catholic." Diana rummaged in her bag for her bleeping phone.

"What?" Jack and Caroline said in unison as they looked at their mother.

"Catholic. His name. Rory. Rory Kincaid. It's Irish, isn't it? St Peter's is an Anglican church. He's welcome to join us if he so wishes." Diana frowned hard at a message on her phone.

"He's not religious. I don't think he'll suddenly spontaneously combust if he steps inside the church. But thanks."

Diana nodded without looking up from the screen.

"I should hope not. It would make a frightful mess, and we wouldn't want the good ladies of the Friends of St Peter's to clean it up. More tea? I'll make a fresh pot." Caroline grinned over the table at Jack as she got up and headed for the kettle. "Where is he anyway?"

"Taken Badger for a walk."

"Not for me, thank you, Caroline. There are flower wars happening as we speak in St Peter's. The Chair of the Flower Club and the vicar's wife are about to engage in mortal combat." Diana continued to glare at her phone.

"Oh, how exciting." Caroline clapped her hands

together in glee. "Daffodils at dawn! Tulip tantrums! The Great Delphinium Disaster of—"

"Thank you, Caroline. It's good to see you appreciate the effort that goes into the Good Friday service. Passions, naturally, run high. Even if it is over where to put the daffs." Diana raised an exquisite brow at her daughter, and Caroline grumbled something under her breath as she finished making the tea.

"We'll gather in the Morning Room at ten-thirty sharp and then make our way to the church." A moment later Diana was gone, vanishing in a blur of pale blue cashmere and a cloud of Chanel No. 5.

Caroline plonked the replenished teapot down.

"Well, that was me told, wasn't it?" Caroline said with no hint of rancour breaking through her good nature. "Poor Rory. He must wonder what he's wandered into. How's he finding it all? A little overwhelming?"

"If that was all, it'd be a godsend. He had a not particularly pleasant encounter with Mum."

"Ah, yes. She told me what happened. She was pretty upset, you know."

"What right does she have to be upset? You know she insinuated Rory's on the make and I'm too pathetic to realise it? I'm a grown man, for Christ's sake. If that was what was happening, doesn't she think I'd work it out for myself?"

"Hey, little brother, calm down. She gave Rory a grilling when she had no right to, but she did it because she's so protective of us all, even though we're old enough to tie our own shoelaces. And she's especially protective of you and always will be, no matter how big a boy you are. You're the baby of the family, remember? And her favourite."

"I'm not her favourite. That's crap," Jack grumbled into his tea. It was his stock response, but he knew it for the lie it was. He *was* his mother's favourite. He knew it, and so did everybody else.

"I don't agree with what she did, but having children myself, I understand why."

"Christ, not you as well. Dad said something similar."

"Did he? Then you should take heed. But you're not getting special privileges, you know. Don't you remember the hard time she gave Tim when it became serious between us? She had him up against the rose bushes. Had a vicious pair of secateurs in her hand and a glint in her eye, he said. Poor Tim. He thought she was about to cut his balls off and chuck them on the compost heap."

Their eyes met. Caroline smiled, and Jack answered with a laugh. His mild-mannered brother-in-law, who wouldn't harm a fly. No wonder the man always had a look of terror in his eyes whenever he was within spitting distance of Diana. At least Rory had bitten back at her, but still. . .

"Look, this is my advice for what it's worth. Ride out the storm. When it comes to it, she won't do anything that risks pushing you away. Her concerns are her own. Whether they're right or wrong, whether you agree with them or not, she's entitled to hold them – irrespective of whether or not they are a pile of steaming bullshit."

"Dad said that as well."

"Ah well, there you go. But I bet he never said bullshit, steaming or otherwise."

"No."

Brother and sister looked at each other and smiled.

"Seriously, Jack. Rise above it all. You and Rory both. Mum realises she's made a massive error. She won't admit it, not in so many words. But she's holding out an olive branch. Rory joining us in church is a big thing. The first time Tim was allowed that privilege was on our wedding day, and even then I don't think she was overly keen."

They both looked up at the sound of footsteps and the clicking of claws. A moment later Badger ran into the kitchen, crashing to a halt against the AGA as he skidded over the stone-flagged floor.

"Rory," Caroline said, beaming. "You're just in time for a cup of tea."

# CHAPTER FOURTEEN

Rory shuffled from foot to foot as he stood outside the age-weathered stone church. Jack was chatting with the curate, as Diana and Roger spoke to the vicar. Short and dumpy, with wild grey-fair hair and buck teeth, he was nodding vigorously. He looked like a frightened guinea pig, and Rory couldn't blame the guy one bit.

He tugged at his collar, unused to wearing a shirt and tie. The navy blue suit fitted like a glove, but under the warm sun, it was uncomfortable, tight, and pulling in all the wrong places. The sudden bellow announced the arrival of Caroline and the Monsters, who both flung themselves at their grandparents' legs.

"Vicar." Caroline's tone was as imperious as Diana's best, and the right reverend of St Peter's answered with a tremulous smile.

"Now we're all here, can we get on?" Roger said.

"Of course, of course," the vicar said. "If you could—"

"Vicar, I have been attending the Good Friday service since I first drew breath. I am fully acquainted with the procedure. If you would be so good as to ready the villagers?"

"Yes, Sir Roger. Yes, yes, of course. Yes." The vicar hurried towards the crowd of villagers gathered on the other side of the lychgate, ready to follow the De Lacy family into church.

*And me.* Rory pulled at his collar again.

"I really do wish Cuthbert hadn't taken up the ministry in Birmingham," Roger grumbled under his breath.

"Roger, please," Diana said, laying a hand on her husband's arm.

"Cuthbert Grimes, the former incumbent of St Peter's. A jolly good sort, who wasn't averse to a tipple or three in the local pub," Caroline whispered to Rory.

"Grandpa's a grump!"

Hugo, or maybe Henry, wrapped his arms around his grandfather's legs.

"Grump, grump, grump," Henry, or Hugo, chanted.

Roger laughed, and he ran his hands through the boy's bright red hair.

Rory felt Jack's hand wrap itself around his own, and he looked up into Jack's enquiring eyes. Rory gave a tiny nod and tinier smile as he squeezed Jack's hand.

"Cake! Want cake now!" both boys shouted in unison.

"I want cake *and* ice cream," chimed one, outdoing his brother.

"Later, and *only* if you behave." Diana glared, stunning the twins into silence.

"Wish I had that effect on them," Caroline muttered under her breath.

"The congregation is ready, Sir Roger," the vicar said, breathless as he waddled up to them.

The family fell into place. Roger and Diana at the head, followed by Jack, with Rory at his side, then Caroline and the children.

"Is this right? I mean, shouldn't Caroline and the boys be with you? I can nip in and take my seat because this is a family thing—"

Jack cut short Rory's urgent whisper.

"Too late for that."

"Welcome to the first of many De Lacy weird and wonderful rituals," Caroline said as breezy as ever.

"When you've quite finished." Roger's deep, serious voice cut off and silenced them before his gaze settled on Rory. "You're more than welcome to enter the church with us, Rory, but if you'd be more comfortable—"

"No. He walks in next to me."

Rory's heart skipped a beat when Jack settled his warm palm on the back of his neck. He looked at Roger and Diana, their expressions unreadable, but Caroline's face lit up in a wide grin.

A moment later, they were making their way in slow, measured steps along the nave before taking their seats on the raised area that was for the sole use of the De Lacys.

The villagers followed at a discreet distance and filed into the pews on either side of the nave.

The small church was soon packed full. Sunlight streamed through the stained-glass windows, bathing the interior in a rich rainbow of colour. The church grew warm, and Rory's fingers itched to pull off his tie and shed his jacket. The vicar's rambling sermon, delivered in a monotone, seemed to go on forever, and Rory struggled to keep his eyes open. Hymns were mumbled through, and readings read by Roger and Caroline. Rory tried to concentrate, but the effort defeated him; he gave up, and let his mind wander.

Rory glanced around, doing his best not to stare at the generations of De Lacys immortalised in marble, paint, and plaques. Soldiers and statesmen, the long-dead favourites of long-dead kings and queens, and the founders of empire. *What would they make of me? Adopted and with no idea who my natural parents were, and who ended up sleeping rough on the streets?* Rory shifted, slipping a little on the highly polished pew, and let his gaze settle on the congregation.

The pews were filled with all ages, and not just the elderly as he'd imagined they would be. Nobody was taking the slightest notice of him, and that's just how he wanted it to stay.

The service ended, the family began to file out of their seats, and Rory followed as they gathered just outside. Rory stood back as the church emptied, the villagers smiling and nodding at the family before scurrying to the village hall on the other side of the road. Some of the older members of the congregation stopped to talk, not just to Roger and Diana but to Caroline and Jack too.

"Well, that's over with for another year, but now we've got the feeding of the five thousand." Caroline nodded towards the hall.

"Sorry?" Rory had no idea what she was on about.

"It's traditional to provide refreshments after the service," Diana said, turning her attention to Rory. "The village appreciates it, and we all muck in with helping to serve up. You'll join us, I hope?"

"Yes, thank you. And I don't mind helping out."

"Then that's sorted," Jack said. "Come on, we'd

better feed the hoards before they come after us with pitchforks."

"Jack! That is not—"

Rory didn't hear the rest of Diana's indignation as Jack grabbed his hand and hauled him towards the hall.

## CHAPTER FIFTEEN

"God, this is foul." Jack forced the dry, stodgy, half-chewed mass of simnel cake down his throat.

"I've deposited mine into my hanky," Caroline whispered in reply. "Even the twins won't eat it—oh no!" Caroline dashed over to where the boys had set themselves up in a corner of the hall, forming shapes with mashed-together lumps of cake.

Jack's gaze swept around the hall. His mother sat talking with a group of women, many with young children on their knees, while his father stood in earnest conversation with members of the local Young Farmers' group. Otherwise, only a few of the villagers remained. And no wonder, Jack thought, if the rest of the refreshments were as bad as the cake he'd surreptitiously dropped in the bin. If he started to tidy up, perhaps they would get the message that the Good Friday tea party was over. Jack gathered abandoned plates, which contained more cake than crumb, and tea and coffee cups, and ferried them through to the small attached kitchen and began washing up, casting a regretful eye over the dishwasher in the corner awaiting a repair.

"Want a hand?"

"What, in the village hall? Mr Kincaid, you are such a tease."

"With the washing up, you dope." Rory laughed as he grabbed a tea towel and began to dry.

Neither said anything for a few moments, the only sound in the small kitchen the slop of water in the sink and the murmur of voices drifting in from the hall.

"You did well out there." Jack nodded over his shoulder. "Were you given the third degree by members of The Ladies' Guild, or The Friends of St Peter's?"

"No. Everyone was unfailingly polite. Chit-chat over tea and cake, all very civilised and English."

Jack snorted. "Don't be fooled. Places like this are a seething pot of intrigue, hatred, jealousy, and lust. All this gentility is nothing more than a thin façade. Haven't you watched any of those cosy mystery things on the telly?"

"Even in Polton Lacy? Never!" Rory exclaimed,

pressing his tea towel-filled hand to his chest and looking at Jack in wide-eyed horror. "Whatever would the vicar say?"

"Don't be fooled by him," Jack said, laughing. "He's the worst."

"Who's the worst?" Diana swept into the kitchen balancing a tray with the remains of the simnel cake; there was a lot of it. She pressed her foot down on the pedal bin lid and chucked it all in. "It was ghastly, wasn't it? I may be a patron of The Ladies' Guild, but I have no say in who they elect as chairwoman. If this is the standard of refreshment we can expect, I might have to exercise some influence next year. It's such a shame Joyce decided not to run for office again; her table was excellent."

"Sorry?" Rory said, looking between Diana and Jack.

"The chairwoman of The Ladies' Guild has the honour, if you can call it that, of baking the simnel cake and all the rest of it. We provide the funds though," Jack explained to Rory. *He probably thinks this is all really weird.* After living a very different life in London for the last few years, Jack was beginning to think so too. "So why can't we ask Anne to do the baking?" Jack asked, turning to Diana.

"You know that's not how it's done. It's an honour

The Ladies' Guild have held for over a century. There would be uproar if—"

"Sheep would be slaughtered and virgins sacrificed on the high moor."

"Jack. These are our traditions. The same traditions you were brought up in, I should add. I would ask that you refrain from mocking them."

"Still horrible cake though."

"Yes, it was," Diana said, her voice softening. "The frightful woman has entered Best Bake in Show, and she's been crowing about her Garden of Eden slice for weeks."

Jack and Rory exchanged confused glances.

"Her what?" Rory asked.

"Garden of Eden slice."

"Oh, an apple cake, then."

Diana snorted. "If only. It's made with tinned tangerines, pineapple chunks, and evaporated milk, among other horrors. Goodness knows where she got the idea. She's convinced it will win her the Golden Ribbon."

"Sorry?" Rory asked.

"The Golden Ribbon. It's awarded to the winner, along with the cup. We don't have second or third places. The winner, as the saying goes, takes it all. Do you think you could help extricate your father from the Young Farmers?" Diana said, turning to Jack. "They've regaled him with the price of feed and have now moved on to organic crop rotation. Rory and I can deal with the washing up."

In other words, Jack thought, I want to speak privately. Given the last time the two of them had done that, Jack wasn't sure if leaving them alone together in the same room was the best idea. Caroline's talk of olive branches came back to him, but it had to be Rory's choice, not his and certainly not his mother's.

"Go and give your dad a hand. We'll get it all sorted in here."

"If you're sure? I'll be outside if you need me." *And not just to help with the washing up.*

Diana settled herself at the sink, taking up where Jack had left off. Rory's stomach knotted and ached, not helped by the heavy cake he'd taken no more than a couple of bites from before discreetly pushing it aside.

He'd barely seen Diana since the encounter in the kitchen, and it was the first time he'd been alone with her since. Rory felt his nerves grinding up a gear; a tea plate, wet from the rack, slipped through his fingers, but he managed, just, to catch it before it crashed to the floor. The silence, save for the swish of water in the sink, was heavy and pressed in on him. But it had been

Diana who'd asked for this, and it was up to her to open the first salvo.

"I fear I may have mishandled our conversation." The rack rattled as she loaded more plates onto it.

"It was hurtful. And wrong." Rory put the plate he'd dried onto a stack on the table, the clank of china against china loud and jarring in the heavy, charged atmosphere of the small kitchen.

"I shouldn't have spoken to you in the manner in which I did." Diana turned to Rory. She'd stopped washing up, but her hands dangled in the soapy water. "But I felt the need to voice my concerns."

"You made them very clear, Diana."

Rory sucked in a shaky breath as he put down his cloth and leaned back against the table. Was this an apology? Was it an attempt at making amends of some kind? She hadn't said sorry, but Rory guessed that for Diana it had never been a much-resorted-to word.

"Yes, yes, I did. But I have to say what's on my mind. I have a tendency to be forthright—"

"When does forthright cross over into being blunt? Or rude?"

Diana winced. "You're not making this easy for me, are you? And you have every right."

Rory pushed away from the table and stared at the cashmere-clad, elegant woman with her hands plunged deep in the grey dishwater.

"Easy? Do you know how easy it was for me to come here? Do you know how easy it was for me to step foot in this world that is as different to mine as you could possibly get? I was throwing up for half the night before we came down because I knew none of this would be easy. Not just for me but for you too. I'm not here to nick the family silver, Diana. I'm here for Jack. I'm here because you're his mum and he loves you, although he's not exactly feeling it at the moment."

"No, he's not." Diana pulled the plug from the sink, her gaze on the water swirling down the plug hole. "I want you to feel welcome here, Rory – whatever you may believe. Perhaps we can take this conversation as a fresh start?"

An apology that wasn't an apology. It was, Rory knew, the best he would get, but if she was offering, he would accept.

*For Jack. Not for me, but for Jack.*

"Yes. I'd like that. Thank you."

He couldn't bring himself to smile because it would be little more than a grimace. They'd formed a truce, and for now, it was good enough.

"If we're finished, I'll go and find Jack." Rory stepped across to the door leading into the hall.

"Oh, just one thing," Diana said, her words making Rory pause. "The family silver was sold off long ago."

# CHAPTER SIXTEEN

"Are you sure you've got everything you need?"

Jack looked at the ingredients gathered on the kitchen table before his eyes flickered back to Rory, who nodded as he checked everything.

After Rory had come to find him in the village hall, they'd headed back to the manor and got changed, shedding suits, ties, and highly polished shoes in favour of jeans, light jumpers, and boots and had gone for a long walk around the estate. *What happened?* Had been Jack's first words as soon as they'd left the hall and were out of earshot of everybody. All Rory had told him was that bridges were being mended, and he and Diana had agreed on a fresh start. Whatever else had been said, Rory wasn't saying, but when he'd emerged, he'd looked if not happy, then more settled, and that was good enough for Jack. Or it was for now.

The kitchen, like the rest of the house, was quiet. It had been a long day for Jack's parents, and they'd retired early to bed, leaving him alone with Rory – and a pile of brownie ingredients.

"Oh, that's gorgeous. So rich," Rory said, taking the tiniest scraping of estate-produced butter and popping it into his mouth. A moment later he was tying the strings of a long apron around his waist.

Jack settled into a chair at the table, ready to watch Rory whip up the brownies for the next day's Easter fete.

Rory weighed and measured, cut, sliced, and stirred. The old, industrial-sized mixer whirred into life, the big balloon whisk combining butter and sticky muscovado sugar into a deep golden mixture. Rory poured melted dark chocolate into the mix before adding flour, mixing all to a smooth batter before tipping in a heap of roughly chopped chocolate, marbled through caramel sauce, and mixed in plump sour cherries from a large Kilner jar. Poured into a tray, they were ready to bake.

"Do you realise you were singing to yourself?" Jack smiled as he dragged the mixing bowl to him and ran his finger around the inside, scooping up stray brownie mix. Jack groaned. *God, this is good.*

"No, I wasn't," Rory said, straightening up from

placing the mixture into the conventional electric oven which sat across from the AGA.

"You were. You always sing when you bake." Jack sucked another blob of mix from his finger.

"Never realised." Rory shrugged, but a light flush broke out on his cheeks.

"How long do they take to cook?"

"About twenty-five minutes."

"That gives us enough time." Jack patted his lap and smiled.

Rory laughed as he straddled Jack. "Enough time for what exactly?"

"This."

Jack pressed his lips to Rory's and was rewarded with a sigh as Rory's mouth softened and opened. The kiss was caramel sweet and chocolate rich, the taste of Rory himself. It was a flavour, Jack knew, he would never, ever get tired of. He shifted, angling his hips upwards, crushing his growing arousal against Rory, who moaned as he deepened their kiss. Jack swept his hands down Rory's back, cupping Rory's arse before hoiking him in closer. Their lips still joined, the kiss grew sloppy, more fevered, desperate, and out of control. Jack shuddered as Rory sighed, the breathy little sound rippling all the way down to his dick.

"Ro," Jack murmured against Rory's lips, pulling back.

The scamper of claws on flagstones and a yelp, followed by the low, rough bark of an older dog was a bolt of electricity, shocking Jack and Rory apart.

"Fuck," Jack growled as Rory scrambled up and threw himself into a spare seat.

"Apparently not," Rory muttered as Badger bounded into the kitchen, followed by the shaggy and lumbering Bruno, with Roger following close behind.

"I thought you'd gone to bed." *Thanks for that expert bit of cock-blocking, Dad.*

"Not yet. We had supper in our room, but we shall do soon. I've come to make a pot of tea. Would you like me to make the two of you some?"

"No thanks," Jack grumbled.

Jack looked past his father to Rory, red-faced and squirming, as he tried to push Badger away from burying his snout into his crotch. Jack bit down on the grin aching to split his face in two.

*Well, dog, you're getting a sight more action than I am.* Jack shifted, thanking his lucky stars he'd dragged his chair close into the table. Giving his dad a glimpse of his denim-clad hard-on wasn't top of the list of things for father and son to share.

*Or ex-hard-on.* Two dogs, a dad, and the offer of a pot of tea wasn't Jack's idea of a turn-on.

"Is that wonderful smell your entry for Best Bake in Show? Diana was telling me how you'd been persuaded to take part. I apologise if you were strong-armed into competing." Roger busied himself with making the tea.

"Erm, yes, it is, and no, I wasn't," Rory said, trying to wrestle Badger's snout from between his legs.

"Badger, behave." Roger's deep voice reverberated around the kitchen, the effect like a hard yank on a leash as Badger jumped back and lay down, whimpering as he pushed his nose between his front paws. "Young dogs have a tendency to be overenthusiastic. That particular young chap is in need of discipline."

Jack caught Rory's eye and grinned.

"I must say, they smell delicious," Roger said, picking up the tray. "Jack was telling me earlier about how skilful you are and the wonderful things you can do with chocolate."

"What?" Rory's eyes widened. "Erm. . ."

"Rory's ganache is amazing. So smooth."

"Really? Excellent. Goodnight to you both. Rory. Jack. Bruno, Badger, come." Roger headed out of the kitchen, followed by the two dogs. Badger paused and looked up at Rory for a second before he scampered off.

"Bloody hell." Rory dropped his head into his hands. "So, erm, you like my ganache, eh?" Rory looked up and grinned.

"I like everything about you—ah, especially your

brownies." Jack laughed as the oven timer began to bleep.

A moment later, Rory was taking them out from the oven and placing the baking tray on the hob.

Jack breathed in deep. The whole kitchen was infused with the rich and heady aroma. His mouth watered, and he licked his lips—and his eyes narrowed as Rory ran his finger around the bowl he'd melted the chocolate in and lapped it from his finger. Jack's lips curled upwards as tendrils of heat spread low in his belly, and his dick twitched. He got up and grabbed the half-full jar of caramel sauce.

"I know you can do all sorts of talented things with chocolate, so now it's about time you showed me what you can do with caramel sauce, don't you think?"

## CHAPTER SEVENTEEN

Rory thought he'd walked onto the set of some cosy TV series set in the depths of the English countryside.

"Is there really a competition for Cuddliest Pet in Show?" he stopped and pointed to a large knot of people, gathered beneath a swinging sign, gripping on to various pet carrying boxes or attempting to restrain small, fluffed-up dogs all straining at the leash to snap, bite, sniff, or mount other small, fluffed-up dogs. Rory spotted kittens, rabbits, and hamsters. And a pot-bellied pig.

"It's one of the most popular competitions. Caroline is one of the judges. I wonder where she is," Jack said, looking over.

Rory followed his gaze, but Caroline was nowhere to be seen.

"The pub landlady won it last year, and the year before that it was Biggles, the primary school pet rabbit. It was about to be awarded the Best in Show rosette when it jumped out of the headmaster's arms and hopped off in the direction of the Best Garden and Allotment Produce tent, where it caused all sorts of trouble by munching its way through a pile of prize lettuce."

Jack was so straight-faced Rory couldn't tell if he was being spun a tale or not.

"I don't believe you."

"No?" Jack quirked his brows.

"Well, I don't think so. . ."

Several people smiled and nodded at Jack as they made their way across the field, some stopping for a brief word not just to Jack but to Rory too. Barely mid-morning, the beer tent was already doing brisk business. The spring warmth and the cool alcohol combined to put the crowds into an easy, happy mood.

"That's the scene of Biggles' crime." Jack nodded towards one of the fete's larger marquees. "It used to be called the Biggest Vegetable competition at one time."

"What, like super-sized carrots?"

Jack smirked. "More or less. The last year it was called that, an old boy from the village won with a giant leek, and I mean giant. It was huge. It probably tasted like crap."

"So what caused the name change?"

"The parish magazine took a photo, with that year's scantily clad winner of a local beauty pageant, which is now defunct, thank God. She was posing with it, and the camera angle made it look very suggestive. When it was published, it looked some promo shot for a cheesy, low-budget porno. The pageant winner renounced her title in a fit of tears and tantrums, and the contest was renamed. Now it's quality rather quantity that matters. Allegedly."

They wandered around, going from stall to stall. Local honey, mead, and cider jostled for space with The Ladies' Guild and the WI selling home-made jams and other treats. Stalls heaped with organic bread and cakes butted up against those offering free-range, local small farm-reared meat. Some of the prices were an easy match for those charged in some of the trendier artisan shops in London. With its coconut shies, tombolas, quoits, face painting for the kids, and an area cordoned off for three-legged and sack races, donkey rides, and a dog agility competition, Rory thought it was a mix of traditional village fete and well-heeled farmers' market.

Seemingly without thought Jack draped his arm over Rory's shoulder. Rory wondered what the villagers might think of Jack's unthinking displays of affection, but if they thought anything at all, they kept it to themselves, and Rory relaxed further into the event and the sunshine.

"Here we are." Jack nodded in the direction of a large marquee. "Best Bake in Show."

It was the largest tent Rory had so far seen as they'd ambled their way across the lower field. They dodged inside, the air cool after the growing warmth out in the field.

Two long lines of tables were set up, and Rory reckoned there must easily have been forty or more. Signs hanging overhead declared designated areas for scones, others for small cakes and buns, traybakes, and another, which was the biggest grouping of all, for large cakes.

"Is that for us, young man?" A round-bodied woman with deep wrinkles criss-crossing her weathered skin bustled towards them and all but grabbed the box Rory held as at the same time she bobbed at Jack. "Master Jack," she said, bobbing before holding up the transparent box and peering long and hard at the contents. "What are these? They're not cakes," the woman barked, glaring at Rory.

"They're chocolate brownies, Mrs Vasey, which is indeed a type of cake. I believe they belong in the traybake and miscellaneous category. Everything is quite in order, I can assure you."

Rory looked at his feet. He looked at the tables,

many already set up with boxes containing what the amateur bakers hoped would be the winning entry. He looked over to the partially open door flap, letting in sunlight and the sounds of the swelling crowd beyond. Rory looked everywhere but at Jack, not knowing whether he would laugh out loud or gawp at his boyfriend. Jack rarely 'put on the posh', as he called it, but his drawl was pure upper crust and cut glass, backed with the weight of centuries of breeding and history.

"Yes. Well, yes, I expect that is the right category for them. Come with me please and sign against your name."

Rory followed Mrs Vasey and signatured next to his printed name, towards the end of a long list.

"Presented and ready for inspection at one o'clock if you don't mind."

Before he could answer, Mrs Vasey rushed over to a couple of new arrivals, each clutching cake tins.

"Did she curtsy?" Rory asked, when they were back outside.

"Not exactly."

"You can't have a not exactly curtsy. She either did or she didn't, and she most definitely did. *Master* Jack," Rory added, his voice dropping.

Jack groaned. "I was hoping you hadn't heard that."

"I rather like it," Rory said, his voice still low.

Jack spluttered, and Rory smiled.

"Maybe I should get out my old riding crop," Jack croaked.

"Maybe you should. Do you have riding breeches, as well, and long leather boots? I want the whole setup."

Jack's eyes widened, and Rory didn't know if it was with fright or excitement. Laughing, Rory grabbed Jack's arm and pulled him towards the 'guess the weight of the piglet' stand.

"Let's just hold that thought until we get back to London," Rory said. *And maybe that riding crop too.*

"Jack! Rory! There you are." Caroline strode over, clutching a clipboard, her face wreathed in worried frown lines. "Thank goodness you're here. I've just had a call from Mrs James, the owner of Pet U Like, the pet shop in Newton Kingswell, to say that she's had a fall and can't come and judge the Cuddliest in Show. I know bugger all about hamsters and guinea pigs," she said, lowering her voice, "and absolutely fuck all about pot-bellied pigs, so I need one or both of you to judge with me."

"Come on, Caro," Jack huffed. "You go for the

furriest, cutest one. It's not rocket science. The clue's in the name: Cuddliest Pet."

"I know that, little brother, but I've got the doctor's daughter with her moth-eaten old tabby staring daggers at the owner of the papershop and her, it must be said, rather mangy chinchilla. I don't want to be solely responsible for the fur to fly, both figuratively and literally, for whichever pet gets the rosette. Come on, boys, give me a hand."

Jack shook his head. "Rory's already been roped into the bloody cake competition, which is enough. Anyway, picking out a cuddly pet can't be that hard—"

"You think? I told you, the fete is World War Three wrapped up in fluff."

"Well, I'm willing to lend a hand. I don't mind petting a bunny and asking what Fluffy's favourite toy is. Come on, Jack, wouldn't you just love to give the doctor's daughter's tabby a tickle?" Rory smiled at Jack.

"No, I really wouldn't," Jack said with a grimace.

"Oh, come on, little brother. Don't be such a grump," Caroline chimed in.

Jack looked between blue eyes and brown, knowing he was already losing the argument.

"Do you really want to do this? I'd have thought the cake competition was enough."

Rory shrugged. "I was always a sucker for a mangy chinchilla."

"For God's sake," Jack groaned. "All right, but you owe me, Caro, and big time. And don't think you're off the hook either, Kincaid," Jack said, glaring at Rory.

"Think of it as reconnecting to your rural heritage. You're stars, both of you. All you need do is ask what their names are and give them a quick stroke. The pets, not the owners. Nodding also helps, as does looking interested. Come on before pet wars break out."

"And what's this lovely little bundle of fluff called?"

Jack looked down to the explosion of fur on the end of the pink sparkling leash. He suspected it was a dog, but he couldn't be entirely sure.

"Demon Seed."

Jack looked from the gum-chewing teenage girl to the dog. It looked as demonic as a ball of cotton wool.

"And what breed is, erm, Demon Seed?"

"Bichon, poodle, and Pomeranian mix."

"That will be why he's so fluffy. They're breeds that are known for their. . . fluffiness."

*Oh fuck.* Maybe pet judging wasn't so straight forward after all. He glanced over at Caroline, a couple of pets and their owners further down the line, hoping she'd see the terror in his eyes and come to his rescue.

*Ask if it does any tricks*, she mouthed back at him.

*And for God's sake, pick it up and cuddle the wretched thing.*

"Does it do any tricks?"

"He."

"Excuse—yes, of course. He. Does Demon Seed do any tricks?

The girl titled her head as she thought.

"If you throw him sausages, he can leap up and catch them."

"He catches sausages? Ever thought of using chops instead?"

"No."

"I was—"

"Oh, what a lovely dog. Competitor number seven, Demon Seed," Rory said, referring to a piece of paper. "Do you mind if I give him a cuddle?"

*Thank God for boyfriends who show up in the nick of time.*

The girl smiled at Rory, who leaned down and petted the dog.

"I'm sure he'd like you to give him a stroke too, Jack. Feel how soft and fluffy he is. And such a cutie."

Jack looked between his boyfriend, staring up at him, and the now smiling girl and back to Rory. *Give the thing a bloody stroke*, his eyes seemed to be flashing at him as he moved aside for Jack.

A quick stroke and pat, then move on.

"Yes, very cute indeed—fucking hell!" Jack snatched his arm back and jumped as the ball of furry cuteness exploded into frenzied, manic, teeth-baring snarling and barking, straining every inch of the glittery leash.

"You've upset him," the girl complained, scooping the writhing dog up in her arms and glaring at Jack. She fished a dog biscuit from the pocket of her hoodie, and the dog forgot its rage as it slobbered over the treat.

"Jack, Rory," Caroline called. "Come and meet Squeaky the parrot. He can do the most marvellous things with peanuts."

"Jesus, now I know why that thing's called Demon Seed," Jack whispered to Rory as he bundled him along to meet Squeaky. "It nearly had my hand off. There's no way I'm touching anything else."

"I wouldn't risk the post mistress's chinchilla either if I were you. The sodding thing got overexcited and started pissing everywhere."

Squeaky the parrot had a repertoire of peanut tricks, none of which involved eating them. Dave the three-legged dachshund was able to leap through a hoop as long as it was no more than an inch off the ground, Gordon the tabby could sing the first two lines of the national anthem, and Pickles the lop-eared rabbit excelled at balancing on an upturned shoebox. Tigger the tortoise was especially impressive, his ping-pong ball skills were really rather remarkable, Caroline exclaimed.

"Ladies and gentlemen, girls and boys," Caroline announced, clapping her hands for quiet. "Super pets, every single one. The Cuddliest Pet in Show is always a hard-fought competition, and this year is no exception. My fellow judges and I will need to take a few minutes to come to our decision, so you have time for a refreshment break."

"Christ, what a shambles," Caroline muttered as she led Jack and Rory to a small table away from the contestants.

"You really have no idea how much you owe me. That little bastard dog was going in for the kill." Jack looked at his hand as though to confirm he still had four fingers and a thumb.

"You got off lightly. I thought Brian the hamster was asleep, but it turned out he'd died. No wonder he was as stiff as a board when I picked him up." Caroline looked down at the pad and scrubbed through Brian's name.

It was a fine line. Tigger the tortoise or the anthem-singing Gordon the tabby. Did Tigger's skill at pushing a ping-pong ball inch by slow inch outweigh Gordon's on-demand strangled mewling?

"Right, so that's decided. Gordon it is. Let's get this done with because I need a drink. Each year, this is what it's all about." Caroline produced a red rosette from a box, with a big number one stuck into the middle.

"Do they win anything else? You know, like a month's supply of cat litter or something?" Rory asked.

"Oh no, nothing like that." Caroline stood, and Jack and Rory followed suit. "But winning Cuddliest Pet in Show guarantees a place in the West of England Pet Parade, which takes place at the end of August, with the chance of becoming the face of Pet U Like for a year. Last year's winner of the Parade is currently endorsing Braithwaite's Worming Tablets. Sadly, it wasn't a Polton Lacy pet."

Caroline strode off towards the waiting contestants.

"Worming tablets?" Rory asked.

"Yes – I think that's what she said. Come on, let's get this done with – and then we can decide what you're going to do as a penance for roping me into this."

# CHAPTER EIGHTEEN

"Is it just Caroline and your mum who're judging?"

"No. The guy who owns the bakery does as well. Cuddliest Pet and now Best Bake. Welcome to rural village life."

"I'm quite enjoying it, in a weird way. It's different, that's for sure."

It was certainly that. Jack cast a quick glance at Rory. His boyfriend was the most relaxed he'd been since they'd arrived. If Jack didn't count being up on top of the Tor, that was. Jack fought the smirk fighting to break out on his face.

*But he does look better.* The shine was back in Rory's eyes, and his easy, ready smile hovered once more on his lips. Most of all, he didn't look like he was just about to bolt. Maybe, when they were back in London, Rory would tell him more about what had taken place in the kitchen of the village hall. For now, if the visit to meet his family was working for Rory, it was working for him.

"Here we are." Jack stopped outside the marquee where the judging for the Best Bake would take place.

It was the most fiercely contested of all the fete's *Best in* competitions. Winner takes it all. No runner up. And no prize other than a coveted ribbon, an old, dented cup, and a chance to appear in a grainy photo on the front of the parish magazine. Friendships had foundered on its jagged rocks. Families had been divided, and reputations had risen like the lightest of sponge and fallen as flat and heavy as undercooked pastry.

Inside, Jack followed Rory over to his table, which was spread with a white cloth. In the middle of the table stood a plain white china cake stand alongside a note with the competitor's name and their entry. And a list of possible allergens, Diana had said earlier with barely concealed scorn.

Jack looked around. Every table had a note: contains eggs, dairy, wheat. . . *but no flavour or originality,* Jack added. Other than Rory's chocolate, caramel, and sour cherry brownies, of course. He breathed in deep. Rory was placing them on the cake stand, and Jack wondered how the tiny morsels could fill the large marquee with such dense, heady sweetness. They wiped out every other aroma, and if there was any justice, they'd wipe out the competition. Jack reached for one and had his hand swatted.

"Ow!"

"Don't mess up my display."

Rory pinned him with a stern stare. It was a look Jack rarely saw, but when he did, he knew Rory meant business.

Tiny square was heaped upon tiny square, forming a jagged pyramid. It was artful without being arty, complex in its simplicity, but most of all the tapering tower of chocolate indulgence whispered *eat me* in a velvet-smooth breath.

Jack pulled his phone out and took a photo. This was the reason Rory not only deserved but needed his own bakery. His talent was too powerful to be kept under wraps. *No wonder Arturo's don't want him baking for them.* The owner and head baker was too stuck in his ways to recognise star quality when he saw it. Or maybe he did recognise it and didn't relish the competition. *Too late now.*

Diana glided up to them.

"My goodness, they look good enough to eat!" Diana huffed at her own joke. She ticked something off on her clipboard with an elegant thin silver pen, which she then wedged behind her right ear. "Judging will start in twenty minutes. Oh dear."

Jack followed her gaze.

The wonky top half of a lemon curd-filled sponge was sliding away, its icing sugar-dusted top reminding Jack of an avalanche building momentum. A second later, the top bounced from the table and landed curd side down on the ground and cracked down the middle. In the flash of an eye, a black-and-white Border collie dashed from under a nearby table, stuck its muzzle into the sponge top, and chomped.

Diana rushed towards the table as a frantic young woman tried to push the dog aside to rescue the half-eaten layer.

"Mr Hemmings," Diana called as she yanked the dog away by its collar, "will you please keep Pepper under control." Her clear voice rang through the tent, stilling everybody mid-cake assemble as an elderly man shuffled across and attached a leash to Pepper's collar and led the curd- and icing sugar-smeared dog away.

"Miss Timms, please," Diana said, her voice hardly any quieter. "That's awfully bad luck, but all entries must be presented in their original state. You really can't reattach the top layer – not that there's much of it left. I'm sorry, but I'm going to have to disqualify you." Diana ran a savage line across her clipboard, impervious to the frantic pleas from Miss Timms. "Brenda. Brenda!" Diana called to a woman over the other side of the marquee. "Please take Miss Timms and give her a cup of tea. She's distraught, and her nerves are quite shot."

A sobbing Miss Timms was led away by the obliging Brenda, accompanied by condolences for the loss of her cake and the promise of the restorative powers of tea. A minute later, all evidence of Miss Timms and her collapsing curd cake had vanished.

"If that's the standard of competition, you've got nothing to worry about."

Jack looked around. The marquee was buzzing with activity as competitors turned cake stands one way, then another, then back to their original place.

"I want the competition because I don't want to win. This is about the village, and that means a villager should win. I'm only here to help your mum and Caroline get out of a tricky situation, that's all."

Before Jack could answer, Diana's voice once more filled the marquee, instructing competitors to stand behind their tables, ready for the judging to begin. Only competitors and judges were permitted to remain. And Mr Hemming's assistance dog, Pepper, who had to remain under Mr Hemming's table *at all times.*

"Well, this is it. Good luck." With a quick kiss and a thumbs up, Jack slipped away.

# CHAPTER NINETEEN

"Before we begin the judging for Best Bake in Show, I want to remind you that the judges' decision is final. If there are accusations which cast aspersions on another entrant, of any description, firm and conclusive evidence must be presented without delay and corroborated by at least one independent witness. I'm sorry to have to bring this up just before we begin judging, but after the very upsetting Bath Bun incident of last year, I believe a reminder is timely. Any questions?"

Silence filled the marquee. If anybody had the questions Diana didn't want or expect, they were keeping them close to their chest. Rory stood behind his table, his back straight and shoulders pulled back. *Hashtag BathBunGate.* Rory fought to suppress a snigger.

"Apologies, just one more thing. My daughter, Caroline, and fellow judge, has had to be deployed to the children's donkey ride arena. There was an incident with Pippin, a super little donkey I'm sure you're all familiar with, and Mr Derek Heath, the proprietor of Del's Donkey World, which has unfortunately led to Mr Heath being taken to the cottage hospital to have his foot X-rayed. Pippin, you will be relieved to hear, is unharmed by the experience and continues to provide the children of Polton Lacy and the surrounding villages with rides around the great oak on the far side of the lower field, with all proceeds going, as you will be aware, to local animal charities. This means that it will just be Mr Walton, who you all know is the owner and head baker at Bread, Buns, and Baps, and I who will be judging this year. Mr Walton, shall we commence?"

A very thin man, who Rory didn't think ever ate any of his own baked goods, nodded at Diana, and the competition began.

It didn't take long for Diana and the village baker to appear.

"Rory Kincaid. A last-minute entrant with his chocolate, caramel, and sour cherry brownie." Diana placed her clipboard down and lifted a piece of brownie onto a fresh paper plate, and Mr Walton followed suit.

"Excellent consistency. Dense without being stodgy." Diana peered at the square of brownie on her plate as she gave it a firm prod with her forefinger.

"The aroma's good," the baker said. "Rich and heady without being cloying. But the proof of the pudding – or should I say brownie – is in the eating. Oh, delicious," he cooed before taking another bite.

"Plenty of caramel and good-sized pieces of cherry," Diana muttered before noting her findings on the sheet of paper on her clipboard. "Now for the taste test."

Diana's eyes widened, just a little but enough for Rory to know he'd surprised her.

*At least I've done something right.*

"Very good," she said, making notes on her clipboard.

"Delicious, young man, truly delicious. Utterly mouth-watering. So wonderfully moist. The addition of caramel sauce is inspired. Succulent. These really do melt in the mouth. If you want a job in my bakery, it's yours," Mr Walton said, nodding his head as he helped himself to another square.

"We need to move on." Diana glanced at her watch. "Thank you for your entry, Rory. Please remain here while we complete the judging. Brenda will bring you a cup of tea."

The woman who'd escorted the hysterical Miss

Timms was already rushing towards him with a cup and saucer from a stack on a large metal tea trolley parked in a far corner of the marquee.

Rory sipped his tea, accepted a top-up, and wondered how long it would be before he could slip away and find Jack.

At long last the judging was over.

"Ladies and gentlemen. Thank you for taking part in this year's Best Bake in Show. With so many wonderful entries to choose from, it really has made our job very, very difficult. But there was one which truly stood out. This year's winner of the Golden Ribbon and this magnificent cup," Diana said, holding aloft the battered trophy, "goes to Mr Donald Hemmings for..."

Rory let go of a long, deep breath of relief. He hadn't won. The prize and prestige had gone to a villager. Nobody could point the finger at the upstart from London who just happened to be Jack's boyfriend and a qualified baker. He'd stepped in and helped out, but now all he wanted was to get out of the hot and stuffy marquee and go and find Jack.

"All entrants over here please."

The man from the parish magazine was calling to everybody to gather around the winner. Photos were taken, and Mr Hemmings made a speech, thanking a long list of those who'd inspired him in his love of baking, before being eased aside. The crowd of village bakers broke up, leaving their various cakes and bakes to be cut, sliced, and packaged for delivery to the local old people's home. It was time to escape.

"Rory."

Diana stopped him in his tracks.

"May I have a brief word?" She nodded him over to a corner.

With no idea what she was about to say, Rory's stomach tightened.

"I hope you're not disappointed you didn't win – even though your entry was by far the best."

Rory hadn't known what to expect, but it hadn't been that.

"It was never about winning. I took part to help you out. But thanks, I'm glad you liked it."

Diana nodded. "I had to tell Mr Walton who you are, and we both agreed—"

"That it could have been awkward if I was declared the winner because of my connection to your family."

"Exactly. And thank you for understanding. Really, the politics around the Best Bake in Show. . ." Diana shrugged. "You're very talented, Rory, if they're anything to go by. I'd push for a baking job in that place where you work if I were you. Again, thank you for agreeing to step into the breach. Now," she said with a brief smile, "I must go and help Caroline with the donkey rides."

Rory watched her retreating back, wondering if she'd still think he was talented once she found out about Jack's plans for him.

He swallowed the thought, and the lump in his throat, as he followed her out into the sunshine.

# CHAPTER TWENTY

"Where's my Easter egg? Where have you hidden it?" Jack slipped back under the bed covers – and put his cold hands on Rory's warm flesh.

"Ow! Your hands're *freezing*!" Rory yelped, pushing himself around. "Anyway, you're too old for Easter eggs. And even if I had bought you one, you wouldn't be getting it after pulling a stunt like that."

"Oh? Well, why don't you warm them up for me?" Jack dangled his hands inches above Rory and waggled his fingers.

"No, Jack. No, no, no. . ."

Rory tried to push Jack's hands away, but he was soon laughing too much to resist as he gave himself up to the inevitable. Instead of cold hands, he got warm lips and warmer kisses.

"Hmm, this is nice." Rory sighed. "And a lot less fattening than chocolate eggs. I, erm—"

"Yes? Do I hear the beginning of a confession?" Jack breathed against his ear, sending a delicious shudder through his body, all the way down to his clenching toes.

"Well – oh, God." Rory's breath hitched as Jack sucked and nibbled his earlobe. How was he meant to explain when Jack was doing *that* to him? "I did buy you one, but – J-*ack*. . ." he murmured on a shaky breath when Jack wrapped his now-warm hand around Rory's thickening shaft.

"You ate it, didn't you? Such a greedy boy, Rory Kincaid." Jack's voice, low and gravelly, in time to the slow slip and slide of his fisted hand along Rory's dick.

*I'm greedy, but not for chocolate eggs. . .* Rory sighed and arched up into Jack's touch.

"Come on, Ro, I'm waiting for your confession. You can only have yours if you tell me what happened to mine."

"I. . ." Rory groaned and shivered as Jack massaged his thumb over the nervy, engorged head of his dick.

"Hmm?"

"I ate—them."

*"Them?"*

Rory made a sound he thought was a squeak, but

he couldn't be sure through his fogged-up brain when Jack increased the pressure and twisted.

"Two. Bought you two. Ate them both—oh my God!"

"What the—?"

The fat, furry body bounded onto the bed, all wagging tail, cold nose, and lolling tongue – which licked its way in a wide stripe up Rory's cheek.

"Bloody hell, Badger," Rory said, trying to push to dog away.

"Has that animal been in here all night? Fucking furry cock-blocker."

Badger answered with a bark and an extra hard wag of his tail, which slapped Jack full in the face.

Rory began to laugh, and soon Jack was joining in as Badger wriggled his tubby little body between the two of them.

"I'm being punished for scoffing both your eggs." Rory pushed the fingers of one hand through Jack's fair hair as he stroked Badger's soft coat with the other.

"Well, you're not the only one."

"What do you mean?" Rory narrowed his eyes, watching the embarrassed grin spread over Jack's face.

"I was going to get yours when we get home."

"After Easter, when they're half price, in other words."

"Which means I can buy you two," Jack said, his grin turning triumphant.

Rory shook his head, trying to look stern but guessing the smile he couldn't stop breaking out over his face put paid to that. He and Jack nestled back into the bed, with Badger wedged in between the two of them.

"This is our last full day before we go home." Rory turned his head to look at Jack.

"I'm sorry."

"What for?" Rory said, frowning.

"For putting you through it. For being roped into all the fete crap—"

"I enjoyed the fete crap, as you put it. Having to make a decision between Tigger the tortoise and Gordon the tabby was edge-of-the-seat, nail-biting stuff."

Jack huffed out a laugh. "You should have won the Best Bake though. If you were the best, you were the best."

"No, it was right that a villager took the prize. Your mum made the right choice. I'm glad she told me, though what she'll—" Rory stopped and swore silently.

"Is there something you've not told me? Ro?"

Rory paused, taking his time to answer.

"I told you she complimented me on the brownies and thought I had a talent?"

"And?"

"Well, she said I should push for a baking job at Arturo's."

"She recognises that you know what you're doing, which is one good thing. But we're one step ahead. I don't care what she does or doesn't think, this is our future we're talking about, and I'm willing to invest everything I've got to make it work."

"Perhaps you should—"

"What? Talk it over with my parents? Seek their views? Ask for their permission? Yes, yes, and no. What I do with my money is for me to decide, not them."

"I was going to say not mention it to them. At least not yet." Rory bit down on his lip and looked away when the intensity of Jack's gaze became too much. "I'm sorry. I—I just don't want to cause any more upset, not when things have settled down."

"Hey, look at me and listen."

Rory peeked up at Jack, relief flooding through him when he saw his boyfriend wasn't staring at him in anger or disappointment. Instead, he saw a steely resolution shining from Jack's blue eyes.

"Do you remember saying we should tell my parents the truth?"

"Yes, but that was about—"

"How we met. I know. But it goes beyond that. I'm

going to tell them about the bakery, not when it's a done deal, but before we leave. I want them to know what we're planning, but I won't let them influence me. My parents aren't stupid; both of them are savvy business people. This estate is only the success it is because of the smart choices and investments they've made over the years. When my Dad inherited, all he got was a crumbling manor and a load of debt. Between them, they turned it all around. They'll recognise what we're doing for the good, sound business it is. And it'll be that because of you. Come on," Jack said, getting out of bed and holding his hand out to Rory. "Like you said, this is our last full day here, so let's make the most of it. We'll tell them about it at dinner later. It'll be fine."

Rory nodded and hoped his smile didn't look as fixed and stiff as it felt as he tried to feel as confident as Jack sounded. And failed.

## CHAPTER TWENTY-ONE

"Mmm, G&T. You can't beat it. Especially before dinner. I put my nose around the door of the King's Parlour before I came in here, and I'm very happy to report that a couple of bottles of Margaux 1989 have been decanted. Monsters! Leave Badger's tail alone." Caroline glared at her two young sons.

Hugo and Henry laughed, Badger barked, and neither the four-legged nor the two-legged animals took any notice.

"So." Caroline turned her attention to Rory. "I expect it's been an education, coming here—and not too bad a one, I hope?"

"Well, it's—"

"Education? More a trial by ordeal." Jack said, cutting off Rory.

The day of their departure was looming, and for the first time ever, Jack was glad to be leaving. The tension had slackened since Rory and Diana had spoken privately on Good Friday, but it was still there in the background like a low-level thrum. And it wasn't good enough. Rory was in his life for good, and that meant he had to be accepted by *all* the De Lacys.

"It's been different. But I've enjoyed it."

"Or mostly," Caroline said, a knowing smile lifting her lips. "I certainly want you to return and as soon as possible. Cheers." She held out her glass for Rory and Jack to clink.

Despite his confident assertion earlier that day that his parents would see the bakery as a good business move, Jack was no longer quite so sure. Doubt had crawled its way in, where it squirmed deep in his gut.

It was a good move, he was convinced of it. He'd quietly and without fuss carried out his homework, talked to the right people, had approached the idea dispassionately as he'd looked at the numbers. It had been difficult to tamp down on the creeping excitement and not to say anything to Rory until he was sure the odds of success were high. He had no doubts, and just as important, neither did Rory, *but*. . . his mother's suspicions of Rory's motives, wrapped up in her overbearing concern, gnawed away at him.

Rory's suggestion not to say anything was tempting. Just wait until the whole thing was a done deal. But Jack couldn't. It felt wrong, even deceitful. He would tell them their plans and cross his fingers they'd be excited for their youngest son and the man he loved. And if they weren't? It was something he'd have to handle. Somehow.

"Jack? Jack? Would you like another?"

"What?" Jack's head snapped up, and he looked into his father's eyes. He'd been so deep in thought he hadn't noticed his parents slip into the room.

"So, what are your observations on rural life, Rory? Has it all been very old-fashioned? Antiquated? Feudal?" Roger said as he sat down opposite the sofa, his brow raised as a smile played around his lips.

Jack glanced over to Diana and Caroline. They'd been chatting but had stopped and were looking at Rory with the same anticipation as Roger was. Jack opened his mouth to head off his dad's question, but Rory beat him to it.

"It is old-fashioned, but good old-fashioned. It's the traditions, I suppose."

Rory tilted his head as he clamped down on his lower lip. It was a sign Jack had come to recognise of Rory thinking hard, choosing his words, mulling over what to say and how to say it. Like his parents and his sister, Jack looked at him and waited.

"There's a connection between you, as a family,

and the village. The whole church thing on Good Friday. I was expecting it to feel, I don't know, patronising or condescending to the villagers, but it didn't. It was like there was a common purpose. Everybody was there because they wanted to be, because it's what the village does. Sorry, I'm not explaining it well."

Jack smiled when Rory, his face growing red, looked at him. His stumbling words had found their mark. Jack's family was the village, as much as the village was the family. They were two halves of the same beating, living heart.

"Well, I think you're spot on," Caroline said, leaning forward and patting Rory's knee. "As late as about twenty years ago, this was an isolated and tight-knit community. Although it's no longer isolated, it's still tight-knit. The traditions *do* appear senseless, strange, and antiquated to those who've not been brought up in them. We all know that, but aren't most traditions when you really take a close look? Many of the families have been here as long, if not longer, than the De Lacys. Our daft traditions bring us together, but they don't bind us. Everybody chooses what they do and don't want to be part of. But you've just had a taster of what goes—"

Everybody looked around as the door opened.

"Sir Roger, Lady Diana," Anne said. "Lunch will be served in the King's Parlour in five minutes."

"Thank you, Anne. Come along, everybody." Diana stood and glared into the corner of the room. "Monsters, Badger is not a donkey, so please do not attempt to ride him."

~

Jack slumped back in his seat. Tender, sweet, traditional roast lamb washed down with a couple of glasses of Margaux '89 had blunted the spikes of what had been, at times, a jagged-edged visit.

They all sat at one end of the long, polished table. The King's Parlour was formal, but Rory, laughing as he and Caroline entertained Roger and Diana with stories of the Cuddliest Pet in Show competition, appeared unconcerned about the chilly painted gazes of long-dead De Lacys looking down from the walls. Jack swirled more of the rich red wine over his tongue and settled further back into his chair.

"Ooooh, treacle tart and clotted cream. My favourite," Caroline said as Anne came in and dished up dessert. "Hugo, Henry, go and play in the Morning Room, not at the table if you please. And leave that blessed dog alone when you do so." Amid squeals and shouts, the two young boys jumped down and were gone in a second, slamming the door behind them.

"This is wonderful, Anne," Rory said, taking a bite. "Have you put ground almonds in the pastry?"

"You'll have to let Rory have the recipe," Jack said, smiling up at the cook-housekeeper, "because this will sell like hot cakes – or hot treacle tart – in the bakery."

The silence that filled the room was punctuated by the door closing as Anne left.

"Have you got a new job?" Diana asked. "Will you now be baking rather than—"

"Pouring coffee and dishing up?" Jack cut across his mother. "He certainly will. We're going into business."

"Business? You're going to be opening a what? A bakers? A café? How exciting!" Caroline beamed at Jack and Rory.

"You're doing *what?*" Diana said.

*Not quite how I wanted to tell them.* Maybe the Margaux had had something to do with it. He took another sip from the fine crystal glass. *No going back now.*

"Yes," he said, meeting his mother's hard gaze. "Rory's wasted in that place where he's working. He's got vision, and he's a talented baker – as you've found out. I've got premises lined up for us to go and look at as soon as we're home."

"It's just a thought at the—"

"Ro, it's more than that." He looked down into

Rory's eyes, seeing apprehension in their deep brown depths.

"Have you taken sound advice? And carried out your research? Spoken to those who know the business – and its pitfalls?" Roger asked, his rich calm voice warming for a moment the chill that had engulfed them.

"Of course I have." Jack turned to his father, meeting his steady, clear gaze. "I—we—are not going into this blind."

"For goodness sake, Jack." Diana pushed her barely touched pudding away. "Cafés, restaurants, and bakeries, more fail than thrive or even survive. Enthusiastic amateurs indulging their hobbies is *not* good business. This isn't an investment opportunity, Jack, it's—"

"It's what?" Jack swung around to face his mother head-on, pushing the words out through gritted teeth. "Come on, Mum, it's what, exactly?"

"Imprudent and ill-considered."

"*What?*"

"Jack, leave it for now. Please?"

Rory's urgent, thin whisper, his hand squeezing over his. Jack heard and felt them both, but there was no way he could *leave it.* Not now.

"Imprudent and ill-considered? For wanting to invest not just in talent and vision but in my, *in our*, future? What do you think this is all about, Mum?

Come on, tell us all what it is you really think it's about."

"Jack," Roger said, "this is not the place—"

"Oh, it's the place. It's very much the place." Jack shot a glance at this father before he returned his attention to his mother.

"Let's just cut through the crap, shall we? Gold digger. That's what you think, isn't it, Mum? You think that, in me, Rory's found some docile, simple fool who's too love-struck to know what he's doing. Well done on getting one right because yes, I may be in love, but it doesn't make me blind."

A heavy silence settled over the table, weighing down as though it were something dense and solid, pushing in on Jack and forcing the air from his lungs.

"No, Jack. That's not what I believe. I had my doubts, but—not now." Diana's face was as pale as the pearls strung around her neck. "But this is a risky venture—"

"For an amateur? Yes. But Rory's not an amateur, is he? This is my idea. It's me who's doing all the running on this. I don't know if you believe me, and frankly, I don't care."

Jack stood and pulled Rory up with him and held up their joined hands.

"See this? It's us, united and going forward. I want your approval. We both want it. Along with your enthusiasm, your thoughts, and your input. But we don't *need* it. I'm angry, Mum. But you know what? I'm disappointed because I always believed you were more than the narrow-minded, suspicious snob you've just shown yourself to be."

"That's enough. The pair of you." Roger's deep, rumbling voice was like the distant roll of thunder.

"Caro, we'll stay with you tonight if you don't mind."

"Jack, you don't have to—" Diana began, but Jack turned away and, with Rory beside side him, turned and left, closing the door to the King's Parlour with a soft click.

## CHAPTER TWENTY-TWO

"That was Dad. He wants me to take a walk around the estate with him." Jack pushed his phone into his pocket and sat down opposite Caroline at her kitchen table.

"In other words, he wants to talk to you in private. You should go. Honestly, Jack, don't walk away from here without making some efforts to make amends."

"It's not me who should have to do that. You heard her, Caro."

"Yes, I did. But I can also hear you. You've got a stubborn streak. In that way you're just like Mum. If the pair of you glare at each other across the ravine, how do you ever expect to build a bridge across it? Somebody has to take a step back."

Jack picked up his tea. Hadn't Rory said something similar, about the need to be sensible and reasoned? He sighed. If his dad wanted to meet and talk, then he'd go along with it. But he and Rory were still leaving straight afterwards.

"Look, make yourself at home here and for as long as you want. I'm sorry I can't be around, but Tim's parents are expecting me and the boys for the next couple of days, and I really can't get out of it. I've put them off so many times I've run out of excuses. Better go, I suppose, and haul them into car. And don't forget to take Badger back to the house. Where is he, by the way?" Caroline looked around as though expecting to see the dog snuggled in the corner of the warm kitchen.

"In bed, with Rory. Again." Jack huffed.

When he'd walked out with Rory the night before, they'd grabbed their bags and Badger had followed them out as they'd made their way towards Caroline's village house. Neither had had the heart to send him back with a hard word as he'd ambled along with them. The Labrador had formed a furry third in his and Rory's relationship, carving out a snug corner in both their hearts.

"Give Rory my love, will you? And don't do or say anything without using that." Caroline tapped his head with her knuckles. "And call me, okay?"

With a kiss and a quick hug, Caroline was gone.

Jack looked at his watch. He had an hour to go before he was due to meet his father at midday at the foot of the Tor. He got up to make fresh tea, thinking about ravines and bridges as the kettle bubbled and boiled and then switched off.

~

"Hey. Dad wants to speak to me," Jack said as he put a mug of tea on the bedside cabinet.

"You are going, aren't you?" Rory asked, looking at Jack as he pushed himself up to sitting. "The way it was left yesterday, it wasn't good."

"This isn't an argument of my making."

"It doesn't have to be an argument at all. Please, try and sort this out because if you don't, everything we do and achieve will be overshadowed by what's happened. Don't make me the wedge between you and your family."

"You know what she thinks of you, and I can't accept that. Ever."

"That I'm after your money? No, that's not what this is about. However misguided and clumsy it is, it's about her doing her best to be a loving parent towards you. Don't knock it, Jack."

Jack groaned. Of course. Parental love, care, and concern – the very things Rory had never had from the Kincaids.

"If I'm going to go, I'd better make a move, I

suppose. I'll see what he has to say, and we'll set off afterwards; I don't feel too inclined to hang around longer than we have to. Will you be all right here on your own?"

"On my own?"

Jack followed Rory's gaze to the window under which a sleeping Badger lay, and laughed.

"I'll be fine. Me and the other man in my life will go out for a walk a bit later."

"We can't take him back with us, much as I know you want to."

"Don't you mean us?" Rory said, a sad smile lifting his lips. His shoulders slumped. "Going to miss him though."

"Yeah, I know. The little sod kind of gets under your skin, doesn't he? Look, if you do go for a walk, take one of Tim's raincoats from their utility room and an umbrella because the weather's on the turn."

"It's sunny." Rory looked out at the clear blue sky beyond the window.

"For now."

"How do you know? Been reading sheep poo, again?"

"Sod off, Kincaid. But just remember. See you later. Love you."

## CHAPTER TWENTY-THREE

"Come on, Badger. Come on, boy."

Rory ambled across the field. He tilted his head and shielded his eyes from the bright sunlight. There was no sign of the turn in the weather Jack had predicted, and when he'd left Caroline's, he hadn't bothered to take the raincoat Jack had advised.

He'd deliberately skirted the De Lacy estate and had kept to the footpaths criss-crossing the field. What was Roger saying to Jack? And would Jack even listen? The last thing he'd ever wanted was to cause a rift between Jack and his parents, but one of the many things he'd discovered about Jack over the last few months was his stubborn streak. Normally so reasonable and willing to see all sides, underneath it all was a bar that would not be bent.

The sun disappeared behind a cloud that hadn't been there a moment before.

"Oh?" Rory looked at his watch. It was late afternoon, almost early evening, and the now cloud-filled sky brought a chill to the air that hadn't been there when Rory had set out almost four hours before.

*How come I've been out for so long?* The paperback pressing against him in the back pocket of his jeans was the answer.

He'd found a shady spot and had lost himself in the book, finishing it before he'd got up and carried on with his walk, but the fiction on the printed page had soon been overshadowed by the real-life De Lacy drama as he'd replayed not just the events at yesterday's dinner but the whole visit.

He needed to phone Jack, to let him know he was on his way back to Caroline's.

"Oh, fuck it," he swore under his breath. His phone, it was in his bag along with the rest of his hastily slung-in things and sitting on a chair in the low-ceilinged bedroom. *Okay, let's get back as quick as possible.*

Rory looked, *really looked,* around him. Badger was a few yards off, sniffing and snuffling around a clump of purple gorse. The lush green field Rory had been walking through had turned to rough upland moor.

Rory shielded his eyes as he searched around him.

"Where the hell am I?"

There was no sign of the village, the manor, or any recognisable landmark. He shivered as a gust of wind blew up out of nowhere, and he wished he'd brought a raincoat after all.

*I can't be too far away*. He cast around, spotting in the near distance the edge of a woodland. The manor was the other side of that, he was sure of it. If he headed towards it, he could skirt around and make his way back to the village. Yes, all he'd done was walk around in one big circle.

The sun came out from behind the cloud, taking away the chill.

"Badger, come on," Rory called, setting a brisk pace as he made for the line of trees, with the young dog walking in step beside him.

"Humpf!"

Rory hit the ground front first, knocking the breath from his lungs. He lay for a moment, waiting for the shock and the slight dizziness to subside before he pushed himself up on all fours and then to standing, holding on to the gnarled bark of a bent and twisted tree.

The wood had been further than he'd thought as he

trudged over the uneven, pockmarked landscape. A gust of wind blew, rustling the branches overhead. The birdsong Rory had heard when he'd first walked into the wood had fallen silent. A fast scrabbling sound made him swing round, his heart in his mouth, but it was only a grey squirrel, rooting through the undergrowth. It stood on its hind legs and peered at Rory before it fled and scrambled up a tree as Badger lunged and barked, looking to Rory to join in the fun and games as his tail wagged from side to side.

"Sorry, boy, but we've got to get going." As soon as he was back, he'd persuade Jack to spend another night at Caroline's. A long, hot bath and a cup of tea, and then, over dinner, he'd tell Jack all about his adventure. The two of them would laugh. Yes, in the cosy warmth of Caroline's home, none of it would seem stupid or dangerous. Or frightening.

*Of course it's not frightening.*

Frightening was a dingy back alley with the street lights punched out. Frightening was walking past a group with their hoods pulled tight over their heads, swigging from cans and bottles, sucking on cigarettes, all eyes on him and the muttered, vicious and sneering words thrown his way. And sometimes it wasn't just words that were thrown. *Those* were the frightening things, not the trees that cast deformed and twisted shadows nor the cold wind that slid around the back of his neck, making the hairs stand on end, and whispering in his ear that he was—

Lost.

"Oh fuck."

Rory stopped. He'd never been here before, he had no clue as to where he was, and with no phone, Jack wouldn't know either.

"What are we going to do, Badger? How in God's name are we going to find our way back?"

Badger wagged his tail in response, his deep brown eyes full of trust that Rory knew he was failing. The wood, silent save for the wind in the leaves, was sliced through with the sharp screech of an owl.

Daylight had given way to twilight, and nightfall lay waiting on the horizon.

## CHAPTER TWENTY-FOUR

"Ro?" Jack called, letting himself in and checking the lounge before he stomped upstairs. The bedroom was empty and silent, like the rest of the house. Rory and Badger had gone for their walk after all.

Back in the kitchen, Jack nursed the mug of tea between his hands. In truth, he was glad of some time alone, to ponder and think. He stared out at Caroline's rambling cottage garden, not seeing the bright spring flowers or the blossom-covered trees as he mulled over the long conversation he'd had with his father as they'd walked the estate.

Jack had expected his dad to try to persuade him and Rory to go back to the manor and to try and understand why his mother had said what she had. He couldn't have been more wrong. Instead, his dad had asked him to talk him through his ideas and plans concerning the bakery.

They'd talked for three hours. Jack had pulled up details of possible premises he had listed on his phone. He'd shown his dad the notes he had from in-depth discussions with contacts, and contacts of contacts. He'd shown him detailed costings and profit forecasts. He'd shown him everything he could to persuade him that what he and Rory were embarking upon wasn't some pie-in-the-sky, ill-thought out idea.

Roger had listened, asking rapier-sharp questions, and Jack had had an answer for each. They'd parted with a long, warm hug. He would speak to Diana, Roger had said, and tell her their son may just have inherited their combined business acumen after all. He hoped he and Rory would call into the manor before they made their way back to London. They both did, he'd added, before he'd headed in one direction and Jack in another.

Jack looked at his watch and frowned. Late afternoon. If he and Rory were going to get home much before midnight, they needed to make a move soon. But where the hell was he?

The bright, clear sky from earlier was filled with dark, billowing clouds. A hard wind rattled the mullion windows, and the low rumble coming in from the high moor exploded in an ear-splitting thunderclap as rain hammered at the glass. The storm had arrived.

Jack poked his head around the utility room door and swore. Tim's waxed raincoats hung from the hooks on the wall. He pulled out his mobile and tapped the speed dial. The sound was faint and muffled, but it was enough for Jack's stomach to drop. Wherever he'd gone, Rory hadn't taken his phone.

Would he have taken Badger to the manor, knowing Caroline wasn't at home to care for the young dog? Maybe he had and was at that very moment attempting to build rickety bridges with his mother, the ones Caroline had told him he should be building.

Jack hit the second speed dial.

Roger answered, and Jack quickly explained.

"No, he's not here. Let me ask your mother."

Jack listened, hearing his parents' muffled voices in the background. A moment later Diana was on the phone.

"Jack? He's not been here, but I did see him earlier in the village. I wanted to speak to him, but he was too far away."

Diana's voice was as clear and clipped as ever. Jack's hand tightened around his phone.

"Where was he going?"

Diana's hesitation was tiny, and when she spoke, her tone was softer and quieter.

"Across the upper field, towards the high moor. Around four hours ago, I think."

The upper field, which edged the rough and rugged moorland, criss-crossed by tracks and paths that when you stopped and looked around appeared to have magically melted away. Fine on a warm and sunny day and if you knew where you were going, but it was no longer warm and sunny, and Rory *didn't* know.

Another crash of thunder as rain beat a heavy tattoo against the windows, and Jack's stomach shrivelled.

"Jack? Jack? Are you there?" Roger's voice this time.

"He's lost. He's up on the high moor, and he's lost."

Wind pummelled the stone walls and screamed down the chimney as the thunder raged in the angry sky.

Roger's voice again. "Get over here. Now."

Roger planted a forefinger on a spot on the map.

*Gibbet.*

"If he carried on through the upper field and onto the moor, that's where he'll be."

Lonely and godforsaken, where men, women, and children had long ago been hanged, their bodies swaying in the wind for crimes real or perceived. Gibbet had none of the bleak beauty of the rest of the high moor; it was wind-blasted, boggy land that had defeated the unwary for millennia.

"We have to call out Dartmoor Rescue," Jack croaked.

"There's no time," Diana said, bending over the map. "The nearest station is almost twenty miles away, and they're undermanned. We'll have to form our own search party. I'll get Fred and Dean. Between us, we know the high moor like the backs of our hands."

"What? Mum, what are you talking about? You and Dad—"

"Will not be sitting here on our backsides."

Jack blinked. "No. No way," he said, finding his voice. "It'll be dangerous out there. The ground will be saturated and boggy. You're—"

"Too old?" Diana raised a brow, as if daring Jack to answer. "Yes, you're probably right." She picked up the house phone. "Fred, we have a slight problem. . ."

"Dad, this is madness. I appreciate it, but it's insane. You and Mum—"

"Know every inch of the high moor. We know every brook, stream, and gully, and every corner of Gibbet Wood as well. As do Fred and Dean. This isn't the first search and rescue we've been involved in, and no doubt it won't be the last. You may have your doubts, but it makes perfect sense for your mother and me to—"

"We'll take two Land Rovers. Fred and Dean in one, us three in the other," Diana said as she hung up the receiver. "We need to get changed and gather supplies. Roger, what about the dogs?"

"No point." Roger shook his head. "They'll never pick up a scent, not in this weather. It's up to the two-legged variety of animal to solve this."

"Yes, you're right. We'll meet outside in fifteen minutes."

Diana turned to go, but Jack caught her by the arm.

"Mum? Thanks. I—I—"

"Jack, thanks aren't necessary, even if I deserved them. Which I don't." She laid a warm hand over his, but when she spoke, it was her voice that was the warmer of the two. "We'll find Rory for you, Jack. We'll find him and bring him home."

## CHAPTER TWENTY-FIVE

"Fuck!" Rory jumped as a huge thunderclap shook the earth under his feet.

Overhead, branches crashed from side to side, defenceless under the onslaught of the howling gale.

*This is Devonshire, in England. People don't go missing here. . .* He wasn't stuck in the middle of a desert, marooned on a mountaintop, or lost at sea in a tiny boat. He'd clear the wood. He'd come across a road or a farm. . .

Rory repeated the words over and over, sometimes in his head, sometimes out loud, where they were ripped from his lips by the buffeting wind. Just a handful of miles away, there were villages, towns, and cities. . . but in the shadowy gloom, soaked by the lashing rain, and freezing cold, and where the only sounds were the wind screaming through the trees and his own shaky, laboured breath, it was growing harder and harder to believe in those places where there was light and warmth.

And Jack.

*Oh, God...*

Whimpering, and the press of a small body against his legs as Badger cowered against him. The young dog's ears lay flat against his head as he gazed up at Rory, all his earlier playfulness gone.

"I'll get us out of this mess, I promise. I don't know how, but I will." Rory reached down to pet the dog, who'd become his near constant companion, and when Badger answered with a soft, damp nose pressed into his palm, Rory couldn't help but smile.

"Come on, we need to get out of this wood. Somehow."

Badger licked Rory's hand, but the crash of thunder that brought a flash of lightning with it sent the dog to his belly, where he lay shivering, shaking, and whining.

"I know it's scary, but we need to go. Badger, come on!" It was hard to inject authority and urgency into his voice when, just like Badger, Rory wanted to cover his head, hide away, and wait out the storm. He gripped the dog's collar and pulled. Although Badger wasn't much more than a puppy, he was heavy, and it was like trying to shift a boulder.

"Badger, move!" Rory shouted, just as another

burst of thunder exploded in the sky above. Lightning flashed, brightening the gloomy woods for a fraction of a second. Dazzled, Rory blinked hard to clear his vision. He tugged on Badger's collar again, rougher this time, and the dog leapt up as if understanding the need to get moving and bounded away from Rory, crashing through the woods.

Rory felt his way. The woods were now in complete blackness, the last of the murky, storm-laden light gone. Every footstep was slow. A misplaced foot and it would be a twisted ankle or worse.

*Just one foot in front of the other, just one step at a time. . .*

Rustling and short, rapid panting rooted him to the spot.

"Christ, Badger."

Rory released a shaky laugh as the dog loped up to him out of the inky darkness. Badger nuzzled into Rory's legs as he gave little, yelping barks.

"What is it, boy?"

Badger wasn't nuzzling against him, he was poking and pushing.

"What are you—?"

Badger leapt forward, just a couple of feet or so but near enough for Rory to see the dog's head whipping from side to side, looking from him, then into the solid darkness and back again. Badger shuffled, almost bouncing on all four legs, and barked.

"Have you. . .?"

Had the dog found a way out of the wood?

*This isn't bloody Lassie, where the dog comes to the rescue. . .* but with halting, stumbling steps, Rory followed, hope rising up in him that maybe it was Badger who was the hero of the day.

Badger's tail wagged from side to side, and Rory didn't know whether to laugh or cry. The young Labrador had led Rory out of the wood but not to a farmer's gate or an isolated cottage but to another expanse of wind-battered open moorland.

The rain had stopped, but Rory felt colder than ever, and tears pinpricked at the back of his eyes. He'd been in worse situations, he told himself. He'd lived on the streets for months, before Jack's act of kindness and compassion at Christmas had come to his rescue. He'd survived those dark and dangerous days, so he was damn well going to survive this. Defiant thoughts, but as he shivered in the wind, Rory wasn't feeling very brave.

"Badger, what are you doing?"

The dog had run ahead and was standing on top of

a hillock. As before he was shuffling around on the spot, the signal that Rory was to follow.

"Oh, God." Rory gasped and cried out as his foot and much of his leg was swallowed up by an oozing pit of freezing cold mud. He lurched to his side, falling hard against a moss-covered rock. He lay there, trying to catch his breath, but the heavy, porridgy mud was pulling at him.

*Trying to drag me down. . .*

Panic was the electricity that shocked him into action as Rory scrabbled to anchor himself to the rock to stop the boggy moor from claiming him for eternity. But the more he pushed, the harder the sludge sucked him back. Taking a deep breath, grabbing at his dwindling reserves of strength as he shoved down on his rising fear, Rory clawed and kicked and dragged himself from out of the bog's deadly grip.

Rory curled into a tight ball, every part of him shaking as sobs wracked his freezing cold body. It was tempting, so, so tempting, to lie there and close his eyes and—the nudge in his back, the damp, warm breath on his neck, and the rasp of a tongue on his cheek was temptation whipped away. Hauling himself up onto wobbly legs, each step slow and laboured and edged with the fear of what was waiting to drag him back down, Rory reached the edge of the hillock and began to climb.

# CHAPTER TWENTY-SIX

They pulled up on the edge of Gibbet Moor. The land was scattered with rocks and boulders and small cairns built up over the years by walkers and travellers, each stone added to the next, a testament to those who'd been foolish enough to pass this way. The rain-soaked land squelched beneath their feet, the spongy moorland pockmarked by pools of sludgy bog, each one lying in wait to catch the unwary.

Like Rory.

Jack wiped away the wetness misting his vision; he couldn't let his dark thoughts take hold when he had to be alert and focused, more than he'd ever been before in his life. Any tears he had would be for after, and he'd make sure they were tears of joy.

The five of them climbed out of the two Land Rovers, and Roger passed around large, powerful torches. Every one of them was dressed in heavy waterproofs, but Jack also hefted a rucksack on his back holding rope, first aid equipment, and a thermal blanket. And a flask of tea, pressed onto him by Anne before they'd left.

Everyone called out for Rory, their voices razor sharp in the still night air. The rage-filled storm had broken up and died away, leaving behind a sky bright with stars and crisp, clear air.

"We spread out, but keep to a line and within earshot of each other. You all know where the danger points are and where the land would have turned to bog. Jack?" Roger's gaze drilled into Jack, who nodded. "Good. We're making for Gibbet Wood. If he's taken shelter, it'll be there."

Fanning out, they made their steady way across the moor, keeping up a constant call. Nothing answered them back.

It felt like a lifetime to reach the small area of woodland, the very last remnant of an ancient forest. They pushed through its weave of knotted branches, picking their way across the uneven, slippery ground. Unlike the moor, there were no patches of bog waiting to catch them out. Instead tree roots and rabbit holes lay in wait. Small animals rummaged and foraged; bats flapped around them, darker shadows on a dark background; and the spine-tingling screech of something small, caught in the talons of a hungry, night-feeding owl.

All the time, they called for Rory. Jack's voice louder and more desperate than any other, before they stopped and listened. Listened for breathing, listened for a small, weak cry, listened for anything that would tell Jack where the one he loved more than life itself lay wounded, frightened, and alone. As he called for Rory again, the only answer he had was his own pounding, racing heart.

"We press on through the rest of the wood and onto Blackwater Pools," Roger called out.

Blackwater Pools. Jack's mouth turned to sandpaper.

Pools of dark water, freezing cold on even the hottest days. A dozen or so, none of them big but all of them deep. *They lead all the way deep into the underworld. . . the devil swims in their murky depths. . . fall in, and the water spirits will pull you under. . .* Jack dragged his hands down his face. Stories told in front of a banked-up, roaring fireplace, stories to frighten and thrill, stories to send a delicious shiver dancing down the spine.

*Fuck it, stories is all they are. . .*

"Jack?"

He looked down into his mother's face. Under the hard moonlight, she looked old and tired, the lines of life etched deep into her skin. None of it overshadowed the strength and determination that shone from her eyes.

"Come on, we need to move through the wood." She squeezed Jack's arm, as sure and strong as her gaze.

"What if we can't find him?" Jack whispered the words that filled him with fear and dread.

"We will, Jack. We will. But we have to keep moving. Come on."

Diana slipped her hand into Jack's and pulled him forward. She didn't let go, and Jack blinked away his tears, thankful she was holding him tight.

~

At the top of the hillock, Rory collapsed into a heap. Everything hurt, everything was an effort he didn't have the strength for. His head throbbed, and his fingers found the sore, tender spot on his temple; they came away sticky with drying blood. Badger snuffled his cold, wet nose into Rory's face, wafting him with his warm breath. Rory didn't push the dog away. Instead he was glad of his presence and thankful not to be alone in the godforsaken wasteland.

"Reckon this is the only time I've been happy to have dog breath in my face," Rory mumbled into Badger's wet and matted fur.

Pushing himself to standing on unsteady legs, Rory looked out over the moor. He screwed his eyes up, trying to make out what the dark smudges were, before he rubbed them with the heel of his hands and looked again.

Water. Ponds or pools. He counted a dozen, maybe more, stretching out as far as he could see over the moonlit land.

Rory's heart crashed. *I should have tried to retrace my steps. I should have tried to go back. . .* But how? By the time he'd realised he'd veered onto the stark moor, he'd already been lost with no landmark to guide him.

Badger barked and sped away, down the other side of the hillock, rushing towards the still, calm water.

"Badger! No, get back now!" Rory shouted, but the Labrador barked as though calling out for Rory to come and play. *Stupid dog. Stupid, bloody dog.*

A loud splash, a cut-off bark, and shrill, panic-filled whimpers.

"Badger? Badger, what—?"

Rory ran forward, slipping and sliding down the muddy slope. His foot caught in a hole, and he tumbled, rolling and rolling, unable to stop, picking up speed, scraping over sharp rocks. The slope was steeper this side, and his flailing arms and legs could do nothing to stop his downwards hurtle until the land levelled out and he came to a stop on the edge of a dark pool.

Battered and bruised, his skin torn and bleeding, Rory lay panting and gasping for breath as he looked up into the star-filled sky above.

*Beautiful, so beautiful. I could lie here and look at them forever...*

Whimpers, whines, and yelps, and the splash of water broke through Rory's dazed, fogged-up mind. He blinked and turned his head, wincing as his neck cricked.

Badger was failing fast, his head dipping under as he struggled to paddle to the edge of the pool.

*It'll be thick with mud. It'll be boggy. It'll be quicksand...*

The words went round and round in Rory's head. It was madness to try and save the dog when he could barely save himself.

Badger's yelps weakened, grew quieter, then ceased. The young Golden Labrador, who'd been Rory's friend, had stopped fighting.

"I can't just... I can't leave him to drown. I..."

Rory pushed himself up but screamed as his ankle threatened to give way beneath him. Pain seared through him, burning through his muscles, bones, and blood. He hurt, he hurt so damn much, but he was still standing

There was nothing, except himself, to save the dog from a slow and agonising death. Badger had done his best to lead him away from harm, and now it was his turn to help.

He threw himself forward and plunged into the waiting arms of the dark pond.

They hugged and held him tight, and pulled him under.

Gliding their torches to try to pick up any clue, calling out, stopping and listening and every time met with nothing, they cleared the wood. Before them was the hillock beyond which were the cold, deep Blackwater Pools.

"On the other side, we'll—"

The loud, howling bark sliced through Roger's words.

"The Pools, they're by the Pools." Jack ripped his hand from Diana's and ran forward, scrambling up the hillock, his boots sliding, losing purchase on the slimy mud.

Badger's bark, over and over, guiding Jack's way.

Guiding him to Rory

*Please God, please. Don't let me be too late. Don't let him be harmed. Don't let him be. . .*

Jack threw himself over the ridge, his legs running out of control, his arms windmilling. By some miracle, he stayed upright as he raced for the dark shape lying motionless on the edge of the largest and deepest pool. Badger hunkered down, pushed up close to Rory's prone body, the barks now only tiny, thin whimpers.

"No, Rory. No, no, no," Jack cried as he pulled Rory, soaked through and limp-limbed, into his arms.

"Jack. . .?" Rory's eyes fluttered open, glazed and unfocused.

"I'm here, Ro. I'm here, and I'm taking you home." Jack pulled him in tight, enveloping him in his arms, rocking Rory's body into his. "I'm here. I'm here. I'm here," he whispered into Rory's water-flattened hair, over and over and over.

The others gathered around them, but Jack didn't care. He didn't care about anything other than the man, the *living* man, he held in his arms.

"Jack, we need to get him dry and warm," Diana said beside him, her clear voice edged with urgency.

Jack hugged Rory with all this strength, resisting her attempt to take Rory from him.

"If we don't, hyperthermia will set in. Jack, please."

Jack stared into his mother's desperate, pleading eyes as hands reached out, loosening his hold and easing Rory from him.

"We have to get him out of these wet clothes and

then get him warm, and quickly. Come on, Jack, help me, for God's sake."

Between them, Jack and Diana stripped Rory of every shred of clothing.

Under the bright moonlight, Rory's skin was as white and cold as alabaster. Rory shivered, so hard Jack could hear his teeth rattling.

*Shivering's good. It's good. It's when you stop shivering. . .* Ripping the rucksack from his back, Jack dragged out the thermal blanket, wrapping it around Rory, his heart reaching for the sky when Rory stirred and moaned.

"Rory! Stay awake. You've got to stay awake."

*Stay with me. Please stay with me.*

"Cold, Jack. So cold," he slurred before he slumped forward onto Jack's chest.

# CHAPTER TWENTY-SEVEN

By the time they got back to the cars, with Rory strapped onto an emergency stretcher, an ambulance and a couple of paramedics were waiting.

Jack had tried to bundle into the back of the cramped ambulance but had been restrained by his father's firm but gentle hand. Let them do their job, he'd said. The paramedics got to work before the doors were slammed shut, and the ambulance bumped its way along the rutted single-lane track and away from Gibbet Moor and towards the nearest hospital, with Jack and his parents following in one Land Rover, as Fred, Dean, and Badger returned to the manor in the other.

"Jack."

The voice was quiet, not much more than a whisper, but Jack was awake in a second, clutching Rory's hand and never, ever wanting to let go.

"Ro? I was asleep. How could I—"

"Because you're tired. If you will go wandering on the moor in bad weather—no, don't Jack, please—"

Jack sagged over the crumpled blankets of the hospital bed. His shoulders shook as loud, wretched sobs wracked his body.

"I thought—I thought—you were—"

"I know."

Jack raised his head and wiped his hands over his wet, tear-stained face.

*If we'd arrived half an hour later, if we hadn't have heard the dog bark, if—*

"Jack, I'm okay. Honest," Rory said, cutting off Jack's wild and raging thoughts.

"But—"

"No buts. Please. I saw the doctor earlier, and she—"

"Why didn't you wake me?" *After everything that happened, how could I sleep through the rest?*

Rory smiled. "There was no need to because I could tell you myself. Get on the bed with me."

Jack climbed up onto the bed and enfolded Rory in his arms. Where were the drips he remembered from the previous night, a night that was seared on his memory but already felt as though it'd happened in another lifetime, to a different Jack and Rory?

"Mild hyperthermia. I needed warming up, inside and out. This is the best way to warm up though."

Jack hugged Rory closer, if that were possible, as Rory snuggled into his chest.

"No lasting damage, and they're discharging me today – with strict instructions not to get lost in bad weather again."

"Should have taken that raincoat." Jack cleared his throat, a tremble running through his words.

"Yeah."

They lay together, wrapped up in each other, the busy, bustling hospital beyond the door kept at bay for the time being. It didn't stay that way for long.

"Can I come in?" Diana's stood in the doorway, looking between Rory and Jack.

"Of course you can," Rory said.

Diana came and sat in the chair Jack had slept in. Jack studied his mother. Always so immaculate, sure, upright, and confident, the woman with rounded, slumped shoulders was a stranger.

Tired, old even, and *un*sure, almost contrite.

Diana clutched at the waxed cotton of her mud-splattered, worn coat. She looked down into her lap. A loose lock of hair, hair Jack had always thought of as golden but, he now saw, was grey and finer than he remembered, fell forward from under the faded silk scarf, fastened in an untidy knot under her chin.

"I'm sorry," she said, her head snapping up. "Rory, Jack, I'm so, so, sorry. I had suspicions and doubts, based on nothing, and it makes me ashamed. I've always told myself I was open-minded, but that's the last thing I've been, hasn't it? All I can say in my defence is I believed in saying what I did, that I was acting in the best interests of my son. It's been made very clear to me that in this instance, mother really *didn't* know best. I—I only hope you can accept my apology and give me the chance to make amends."

Diana stood, and to Jack, it seemed as if it took the very last of her strength and reserves.

"Mum."

"Diana."

Different words for the same woman, spoken at the same time.

"Diana," Rory said, easing himself out of Jack's arms and sitting up. "I understand why. I really do. But you've got nothing to worry about, not about me, I promise you."

Rummaging through a pocket for a paper tissue, Diana bowed her head. When she looked up, her eyes were red-rimmed and glassy. Jack's heart broke. The woman he'd been prepared to walk away from had been the woman who'd trudged across a cold, bog-riddled, dangerous moor; she'd done it willingly not just for Rory but for him too.

Jack slipped from the bed and wrapped his arms around his mother, smaller, thinner, and more fragile than he'd ever known.

"Thank you. Thank you so much," Jack whispered.

Diana nodded. Nothing more, for now, needed to be said. The bridge across the ravine was firm, safe, and solid beneath his feet.

"If you can put off returning to London later today, come home to the manor. Please?" Diana said, her eyes flickering between Jack and Rory.

"We will. We'll come home." Rory smiled, and Jack's heart clenched at the happiness he saw shining from Rory's deep brown eyes.

Home. Jack sniffed, blinked, and blinked again. Rory was coming home, but not just to him.

The love of family, open-hearted and unconditional, everything Rory had craved throughout his life but had been denied, had finally slung its arms open wide. But this wasn't any family, it was *his* family, *Jack's*, and now it was Rory's too.

*We're home, Ro, we both are.*

# EPILOGUE

## EIGHT MONTHS LATER

Rory stood in the centre of the shop and looked around. *Had all this happened in just a few short months?* His arms held too many bruises from the number of times he'd pinched himself to remind himself it was true.

He was alone, for now, but that wouldn't last long, and Rory savoured the moment, savoured the silence as he wondered at what he and Jack had achieved.

Of all the premises Jack had lined up for viewing, it was this place that had sung to Rory. The small square was tucked away behind a busy main road and the closed-up shop that would be reborn as The Bakehouse sat on one corner.

*Away from the main road? Are you sure?* Jack had

asked. And he was sure. Rory had never been surer about anything. Except for Jack, because nothing could ever be surer than Jack.

The square was no further than a twenty-minute walk from their home. Late Regency and early Victorian houses hemmed in all four sides, and in the middle was a small public garden. Brimming with plants of all kinds, with brick-paved paths running this way and that, funky pieces of original art peeked from behind trees, nestled in their branches, or lay half-hidden by bushes.

The garden may have been bohemian and arty, but the hippy vibe didn't extend to the homeowners, not if the big, shiny, four-wheeled drives, interspersed with the odd sports car, was anything to go by. Or maybe hippies have gone up in the world? Rory had thought when he'd taken a walk around the square after he'd first viewed the shop. He'd left Jack talking with the commercial estate agent, telling them he needed a moment alone. Jack had smiled but said nothing. Less than half an hour later, Rory had returned and told them he wanted to sign on the dotted line.

The door opened and Jack appeared, bundled up in a heavy coat, scarf, and hat, and dusted with fresh, feathery flakes of snow.

"You were miles away," Jack said, coming over and resting his hands on Rory's shoulders. "Excited?"

Rory nodded. "And nervous as hell. Our opening day, and it has to snow. It might deter people from coming. What if nobody turns up? What if we're the only ones—?"

"Hey, come on. That is *not* going to happen. The people who live around here are desperate for us to open up. Don't you remember how enthusiastic they were when we did that pre-opening taster evening? You've already got private orders for your brownies, the gin and tonic cupcakes, and—"

Rory groaned. "You really are making me eat my words, aren't you?" What had he said, months before about fancy cupcakes and their weird flavour combos? A late night and a slightly drunken experiment in the kitchen had resulted in the odd-flavoured frosting that had turned out to be a triumph. Something else had turned out to be a triumph too with the pair of them ending up naked and confection-covered on the floor. Jack had said it was a sign and insisted they be included, alongside the carrot cake and the treacle tart. And the brownies, of course.

Jack curled his arm around Rory's waist. "It looks wonderful. It's a little piece of Christmas magic."

Rory's throat closed up. That was exactly what it was. He blinked to clear his suddenly watery vision.

The counter was piled high with delicious bakes and cakes, savoury and sweet. Retro and even antique cake stands, many unearthed from storerooms and back cupboards from Jack's parents' homes in Devon and London lined the counter. Under their glass domes were fudge cake, lemon cake, vanilla and cherry cake, ginger cake. . . nostalgia with a twist, Jack had said. In the centre and heaped up high on the largest stand sat a stack of cocoa-dusted chocolate, caramel, and sour cherry brownies.

Gold and silver stars, angels, reindeers, and Santas hung from the ceiling, no two the same. The mishmash could have been a mess, but somehow it worked, and Rory wasn't quite sure how or why; all that mattered was it did. Ice-blue fairy lights draped the large mirror that ran the length of the wall opposite the counter. *To give the illusion of space*, Jack had said. They'd rejected the idea of bringing in an interior designer and had spent late evenings and long weekends working together, happy to be doing it themselves, and making Rory's vision come alive.

*But not just my vision.*

Jack had discovered a hitherto unknown talent for decoration and design, and he'd thrown himself into the project, often surprising Rory (and himself, Rory thought with a smile) that his unorthodox ideas worked. Reflected in the mirror, Rory caught sight of the doll, taking pride of place on a shelf behind the counter. Doris the drag queen Christmas fairy, decked out in her sequined dress, bright yellow hair piled on top of her head. Jack had plucked Doris from the top of their tree at home. *For luck*, he'd said, as he arranged the old and battered doll on the shelf, on top of a cushion of rainbow feathers. Doris the drag queen fairy had been one of Jack's Christmas traditions years before they'd met. Now she was *their* tradition.

"It's a year," Jack said, his voice quiet in the still air.

A year to the day since Rory had found shelter on Jack's doorstep. A year to the day when his life had taken a turn he thought could only happen in fairy tales. Jack hadn't mentioned it until now, and Rory had kept silent. It was for the best, he'd told himself. Look forward, not back. Today was about the future, their future.

Jack delved into the deep pocket of his old waxed coat. He opened his clenched fist to reveal a plain dark box and stared at Rory in silence.

*A good luck gift, that's all it is.*

Jack had showered him with little gifts as the bakery had taken shape. Often silly, funny things. Sometimes not. Rory's heart pounded, knowing without knowing that whatever lay within the box was a *sometimes not*. His gaze flickered up to Jack's, meeting his man's blue eyes.

"Open it."

With trembling fingers, Rory lifted the box from

the centre of Jack's palm. The top tilted back to reveal a plain pale gold band.

"Jack—?"

"Marry me."

Rory couldn't speak. He couldn't breathe. He couldn't think beyond those two words.

*Marry me.*

Jack took the box and lifted the ring from its silk cushion, looking to Rory for permission.

"Ro?"

Rory nodded, the only answer he could give. It was enough for Jack as he slipped the ring onto Rory's finger.

"I love you so much, Ro. Never, ever forget that."

Rory's eyes drifted to a close as Jack brushed his lips to his in a soft, warm kiss. No raging heat, no frantic precursor to anything more, the kiss was an affirmation of who they were and what they were to become.

The banging on the door pulled them apart, ripping them from their bubble with the unruly reminder that the world around them was still spinning and turning and that life was being lived beyond the locked door of The Bakehouse.

Jack's parents and Caroline pressed their faces to the window, smiling and laughing and waving their hands. They wouldn't miss the opening for the world,

Diana had told them both. Behind them, a small crowd had gathered, increasing in size as more and more joined as the snow began to fall in earnest.

"This is it. You ready?" Jack asked as he took Rory's hand in his.

"I'm not sure. Suddenly it's all—"

"Real?"

Rory nodded. Yes, it was real. And that was just how he wanted it to stay.

"Go and let them in. This is your moment, Ro."

Jack stepped back as Rory stepped forward, hesitating for a second and throwing Jack a nervous smile over his shoulder before he sucked in a deep breath and unlocked and opened the door, not just to let in the milling crowd, but to let in a new life.

*Our life.*

# ABOUT A E RYECART

Thank you for reading, I hope you enjoyed **An Easter Promise** as much as I enjoyed writing it. If so, I'd appreciate it if you could spend a minute or two to post a short, honest review. I'm an indie author and reviews are vital, they really are our life blood.

Why not sign up to my mailing list? Each month, I send out an up-date on what I'm working on, books I read and recommend, events I've been to, and all kinds of nuggets I think you might be interested in. If you want to hop on board (and you can jump ship at any time by unsubscribing) as a thank you I'll send you a free 13,000+ word story.

You can sign up at:
aeryecart.com

You can also connect with me here:
www.facebook.com/aeryecartauthor
twitter.com/aeryecart
instagram.com/aeryecart

## Just a little about me. . .

I love all kinds of MM romance and gay fiction, but I especially like contemporary stories. Born and raised in London, the city is part of my DNA so I like to set many of my stories in and around present-day London although An Easter Promise bucks the trend! I write at home, in the gym, in cafés - in fact any place I can find a good coffee!

## ALSO FROM A E RYECART

## CONTEMPORARY GAY ROMANCE SERIES

### BARISTA BOYS

Danny & Jude

Stevie & Mack

Connor & Ash

Bernie

### DEVIANT HEARTS

Captive Hearts

Radical Hearts

Perilous Hearts

### URBAN LOVE

Loose Connection

The Story of Love

Corporate Bodies

## RENT BOYS

Release

*All series novels can be read as stand alones*

## HOLIDAY & SEASONAL

A Kiss Before Christmas (Rory & Jack #1)

Company for Christmas

## STAND ALONE

Imperfect

Printed in Poland
by Amazon Fulfillment
Poland Sp. z o.o., Wrocław

53795110R00125